"Get down!"

Tanner shut the trailer door and bolted it.

Mara fell to her knees. Bullets sprayed through the trailer windows, chips of glass biting into her scalp. She'd not heard snowmobiles. They must have come on foot.

Tanner yanked his weapon free. He popped up and fired through the fractured glass as another hail of bullets slammed in, gouging holes in the cupboards and tattering the curtains. The blast pierced her eardrums.

Tanner gestured to Britta, and she belly crawled over to Mara. "Take Britta and go out the back. Get away from here."

"Not without you."

* * *

Pacific Northwest K-9 Unit

Dana Mentink is a nationally bestselling author. She has been honored to win two Carol Awards, a HOLT Medallion and an RT Reviewers' Choice Best Book Award. She's authored more than thirty novels to date for Love Inspired Suspense and Harlequin Heartwarming. Dana loves feedback from her readers. Contact her at danamentink.com.

SNOWBOUND ESCAPE

DANA MENTINK

LOVE INSPIRED SUSPENSE
INSPIRATIONAL ROMANCE

Special thanks and acknowledgment are given to Dana Mentink for her contribution to the Pacific Northwest K-9 Unit miniseries.

LOVE INSPIRED® SUSPENSE
INSPIRATIONAL ROMANCE

PLEASE RECYCLE
THIS PRODUCT IS RECYCLABLE

Recycling programs
for this product may
not exist in your area.

ISBN-13: 978-1-335-59768-7

Snowbound Escape

Love Inspired
22 Adelaide St. West, 41st Floor
Toronto, Ontario M5H 4E3, Canada
www.LoveInspired.com

Printed in U.S.A.

Wait on the Lord: be of good courage,
and he shall strengthen thine heart: wait, I say, on the Lord.
—*Psalm* 27:14

To Donna and Mike in Florida. You bless my life.

ONE

The sound of shattering ice yanked Mara Gilmore from an uneasy sleep. She lunged from the bed she'd fashioned from a flattened cardboard box and fell to one knee on the splintery wood floor. A patch of ice caused by the leaking roof made her slip as she scrambled upright. She clutched her fists to her pounding heart. *Just an icicle falling. It isn't him. It couldn't be.* She'd been careful, agonizingly so. Covering her snow prints as best she could. Staying away from the main roads that led visitors around the lower pastures shrouding Mount Rainier National Park. Stuffing her mane of overgrown hair under a fraying knit cap. He couldn't have tracked her. Could he? Not when she was so close to rescue.

She strained to sort through the sounds of the storm howling around the abandoned structure that might have been a vacation cabin in its better days. There was no way to pick out the approach of an intruder from the cacophony. Helplessness left a bitter taste in her mouth.

It's not him. Tears welled in her eyes anyway. She was exhausted from running, her body battered by cold and hunger, weakened by seven months of living as a fugitive. Not just a fugitive from the law, but on the run from the two predators stalking her since the moment she'd witnessed a double murder back in April.

The scene replayed itself in detail in her nightmares. Eli Ballard standing over the bodies of her ex-boyfriend Jonas and his new love, Stacey Stark, Jonas's hand twitching one last time, outstretched as if he'd been trying to protect the woman dying next to him. Most chilling of all, Eli had lowered the weapon, looked right at Mara as he flung her bracelet in the bushes, threw his head back and laughed. She had no idea how he'd stolen her bracelet. He'd set her up so smoothly she hadn't seen it coming.

As if that wasn't damaging enough, her fellow Pacific Northwest K-9 Unit officers had witnessed her there bent over the bodies, hand outstretched to check for pulses. Another nail in her coffin.

And you ran. You confirmed your guilt in their minds, Mara. That's on you.

A crunch from outside smacked her back to the present. She forced down the scream building in her throat. Was the noise made by a pile of snow sloughing off the damaged roof? The logical side of her brain, the one that made her perfectly suited to be a crime tech for the PNK9, a specialized team of police officers and their K-9 partners assigned to the three national parks in Washington State, could not override the fear. She was in danger. Moments away from death, possibly. Unless she was letting her fear carry her away.

The keening wind rattled the warped walls as she quickly shoved a granola bar and the half-empty bottle of water into her pack. Why had she stupidly laid them on the remains of the shelf anyway? To trick her mind into thinking she was actually going to be safe for a few days? A mental retreat from her ragged existence? *Should have left everything packed. You won't be safe until you're back in Olympia. Not a moment before.*

Chiding herself for her foolishness, she looped the backpack over her shoulders. Run or stay? If she could wait it out until daylight, she'd be much less likely to fall on the ice or die of exposure in the raging storm. The tiny abandoned cabin she'd found was a good ten miles from the border of Mount Rainier National Park, but the whole area was rugged and treacherous. The volcanic mountain itself stood sentry over the surrounding valley, cloaked by ancient, untouched forests. It was breathtakingly gorgeous, and deadly. Normal winter snowfall had been compounded by a vicious storm system which had paralyzed the whole region for a week. Howling wind and hammering sleet would prevent Eli from finding her, she told herself, unless the conditions killed her first. And Eli had recruited help. Two against one.

With meager supplies and no means to track the weather, how long would she last in the open? Once she set foot out of the cabin, there was no surety that she'd find another shelter before she froze to death. She'd made a mistake coming here, one of many, but she'd been drawn to the spot because it had been her father's favorite place to camp, a reminder of why she was doing this—running. To save her father.

The ugly reality rose before her like an attacking bear. Eli Ballard was likely out there, or the accomplice he'd hired to track her and they'd left her two choices: run or die.

Decisions used to come so easily to her when she'd had the false notion that she was in charge of her own life. She thought fleetingly of her PNK9 colleagues, tasked with assisting in the investigation of difficult crimes in Washington's national parks. She'd been so proud to be on board, even though she'd always stood a step outside the tight-knit team. Some of them no doubt interpreted her reserve as standoffishness, arrogance even. Still, maybe she should have turned herself in at the murder scene, trusted that justice would win out.

But Eli had made it clear with the photo he'd texted that her father would be hurt if she breathed a word.

Besides, there was too much evidence against her.

And too few friends to have her back.

And trust wasn't something that came easily to twenty-four-year-old Mara.

But they believe you now. What good did that do? She'd heard the blessed news that the team had become convinced of Eli's role in a gun smuggling operation, that Stacey, his business partner, may have found out about it and confronted him, and so he'd killed her—and her boyfriend. They were bringing him in for questioning and he'd bolted. Now that everyone knew the handsome charmer was a snake underneath, it was just a matter of time before they could prove he'd committed the murders too. Very recently, Mara had called her half brother, Asher, an officer with the PNK9 unit, and told him she'd seen Eli gun down two people. He seemed to believe her, but she couldn't prove anything.

The wind howled along with her thoughts. Eli being a suspect wasn't going to save her now, stuck in the snowy patch of wilderness she'd chosen, cut off from help, her enemies closing in. Mara had given her brother a hint about where she was holed up, but Asher was far away. Eli was coming for her, and he had nothing to lose.

You made your bed, Mara. Now try and live to sleep in it another night. Run, she decided, but when? Could she wait for daylight to bolt?

Half crawling, she crept inch by inch to the front door. The cold sliced right through the jacket she'd spent five dollars on at the thrift store in Olympia, the first stop on her frantic flight from the murder scene. Another blast of wind buffeted the tiny structure. The nastiest storms didn't typically arrive in November, this close to Thanksgiving, but nothing had been typical for Mara since that April day when her life blew up. She thought for a moment of Tanner Ford, the quiet dark eyed officer whom she'd almost decided to trust with her suspicions about Eli.

Almost doesn't count.

And he wouldn't have believed you anyway.

A quiet crunch made her pulse thunder, closer now. Nature? Or a human predator?

Where was the noise originating? Behind the woodpile? But might it be an animal looking for shelter just as she had been two nights ago? She wished she could turn on the cheap flashlight, but she'd be signing her own death warrant if it was Eli out there. Gingerly, she eased across the floor, past the boarded-up windows, avoiding the gaping hole that she suspected was being used as a burrow by a marmot family. There was no window in front, but the door was so badly weathered there was a sizable chink at the bottom. Breath held, she knelt and put her eye to the spot.

Blinking, she could pick out only the flakes whistling by in lacy sheets.

Maybe she had nothing to be concerned about? The thoughts died away as she spotted a shifting shadow that was not that of a tree or animal. Someone was approaching up the walkway now, one carefully placed footstep at a time. A burly figure, swathed in thick snow pants and jacket. Short and squat... Eli's accomplice.

Terror piled up inside her like a massive snowfall.

The back door. It was her only chance. She rushed to her cardboard box bed and pulled on her boots. The window boards were nailed firmly in place but there was a gap between two of the warped slats. Freezing cold lasered her as she peeked out.

An eyeball stared back at her through the gap. Shock drove her stumbling back. The eye retreated slightly. She saw only a tiny sliver of face, the gleam of an eyebrow. She knew that face, that smile, the same one she'd seen the day that changed everything.

"Little pig, little pig, let me in." Eli Ballard's laugh was colder than the blizzard.

Eli's man was on the front step and Eli himself was waiting for her in the back...both escape routes blocked.

Trapped.

She looked frantically around for something to use as a weapon. A broken slat stood in the corner, the remnants of a chair perhaps. With shaking fingers she snatched it up.

Two strong men against a woman with no protection.

All right, Mara. It's do or die time. Whispering a prayer, she gripped the wood and waited.

PNK9 officer Tanner Ford eased slightly to the right to quiet the pain from his healing gunshot wound. It didn't help that his limbs were frozen slabs of meat. His winter gear barely deflected the cold. Frigid wind ripped his face as he focused the night vision binoculars on the cabin. Britta, his K-9 boxer, remained tense, her whip of a tail wagging. She seemed impervious in her zip-up vest and booties.

Britta was certain who was inside that cabin, even if Tanner wasn't. His dog had tracked Mara's scent for miles from the fishing cabin where she'd holed up two days earlier. Asher Gilmore, Mara's half brother and Tanner's one close friend, was positive he'd find her there.

"She gave me a clue on the phone before we were disconnected," Asher had said. "Dad's favorite spot, a place from her childhood where my father used to take her." Tanner had registered the disdain shading the word *father.* "You've got to get her out before Eli finds her. Britta's the only tracking dog available and you have rock star wilderness skills."

"Flattery will get you nowhere," he'd said, but knowing Mara was in grave peril had launched him into the rescue mission without hesitation. Thanks to Britta, he was optimistic they'd found her, with enormous effort, just as a blizzard completely cloaked the tiny bowl of a valley. If he was wrong about her being inside, he'd need to find out soon and trek back to his vehicle before they both got hypothermia or frostbite. Each moment he lingered intensified the risk.

Britta shoved at him with her flat nose as if to say, "I know what I'm doing. Let's go get her already."

But something wasn't right. His instincts screamed at him, fingers numb around the binoculars in spite of the gloves. He refocused the lenses. A sound told him what his eyes couldn't, the thud of a boot slamming against a door.

Eyes tearing, he zeroed in on the front porch through the deluge of snow. He could barely pick out a tank of a guy battering the wood. One more kick and he'd be through. *Showtime.* Tanner leaped from his snowy platform and plowed down the slope, pulling his weapon. "Police," he yelled as loud as he could above the tumult.

The man whipped around and freed a weapon from his pocket, firing.

His pulse went into overdrive as he shouted, "Down, Britta."

His K-9 partner flattened herself at his side. He rolled behind a snow-covered tree, Britta taking cover beside him. He aimed with care lest his bullet plow right through the fragile cabin walls.

The guy fired off two more shots, then stopped. Breath hitched, Tanner poked his head around the tree. The man yanked a snowmobile from behind a pile of rock and zoomed away. The snow fell in clumps as he and Britta crept from their hiding spot. He stayed low, hurrying to the cabin door, Britta silent and tense at his side. He had no idea what he was about to find. Mara? Eli? He pushed a palm against the door and met resistance. Fastened from the inside.

Plan B. Edging off the porch, he and Britta crunched gingerly around the periphery of the weather-beaten structure. When they paused at the corner Britta stiffened, barking once. Her bark lit up his nerves and he hit the ground next to her as Eli Ballard reeled around the corner firing. The shot would have taken off Tanner's head if Britta hadn't alerted him. Eardrums throbbing, Tanner attempted to return fire from his prone position, but Eli kept going. Britta barked at a deafening level at Tanner's side. She was not a protection dog, her specialty was tracking and trailing, but she would defend him if she could as she'd tried to do when he'd been shot back in August. Tanner scrambled upright, slipped on the snow and went down hard on his knee. She nosed him anxiously. By the time he got up, Eli was out of sight.

"That didn't go to plan." He swiped the snow from his face. There had been no sound that he could tell from the cabin, but he wouldn't have heard anything anyway, over the storm. He looked to Britta who cocked her head, ears twitching. She sat. Her signal. Mara was inside. Alone? Hurt? Worse? He stood and peered through the crack between the slats, but the interior was dark.

"Mara?" he called softly.

No answer. No movement.

"It's Tanner Ford with the PNK9," he said louder. The wind snatched his words away.

He couldn't delay much longer in the bitter cold. "Here goes nothing." After a command to Britta to stay, he yanked off the window board and leaped through the opening in one swift movement. He landed on his feet, the wood groaning beneath his weight.

The gloom inside didn't reveal much.

"Mar..." He didn't get the last syllable out before something rushed at him. He caught the briefest movement of a club or stick raised in the air. The weapon crashed into the door frame as he reeled aside. Stumbling back, he raised his arm to avoid the second blow which narrowly missed his shoulder. Britta was barking all out now, head thrust through the window gap.

He got a glimpse of heavily lashed eyes, a petite face. His attacker wore an incongruous pom-pom hat. She raised her hand to swing again, eyes unfocused and wild.

"Mara," he got out. "It's Tanner Ford."

His words finally penetrated. He heard her gasp and she dropped the stick and fell to her knees next to him. "Tanner?" She panted. "I'm so sorry. Did I hurt you?"

"No, but that was an all-star–worthy swing." He sat up and gave Britta a hand signal to enter. The dog leaped through the window, first checking on him and then inserting herself in Mara's arms. She buried her face in the dog's silky neck. "Oh, Britta. I missed you so much."

Britta, it seemed, had not forgotten the woman who used to bring her special treats and hung out with her when Tanner was plowing through paperwork. Mara looked different now, thinner, her eyes filling with the gleam of tears, cheeks hollow. So young, twenty-four to his thirty-four. Maybe the circumstances made her seem younger than he remembered.

"You found me." He wasn't sure if she was talking to him or Britta. "I didn't think I'd live long enough to get back home." Tears ribboned her cheeks and her body quaked. "Eli killed them… Stacey and Jonas… and he's been after me."

He reached out a hand. Her fingertips were cold, impossibly small in his grasp. They got up. "Asher shared what you told him. We have proof about Eli's smuggling. We'll get him for double murder too, but that'll need more solid evidence and your eyewitness account. Glad you're okay, but we can't stay here."

She hugged herself, her body slight under her puffy patched jacket. What had she been through the past seven months? There was no hysteria in her voice when she answered, though. "I agree. He's out there, with his hired guy. He won't give up for long."

Tanner nodded and started to jog to the front of the cabin, but Mara snagged his wrist and pointed to the floor. "Watch out for the hole."

He sidestepped. "Thanks. Saved me a broken ankle."

"Least I could do." Her shaky smile teased one from him.

"My car's parked about two miles up the road. It was snowing hard when I got here so I'm not sure we'll be able to drive out, but I brought supplies and I can radio from there." Through the gouge under the door, he did not see any sign of either of the two men.

But they could easily be hiding. Waiting for another chance. He looked again at Mara. She was shivering.

"Do you have anything warmer to wear?" He pointed to the hole in the collar of her jacket. Ridiculous question, probably.

She shook her head. "I'm wearing everything I have."

Everything? How had she not fallen victim to hypothermia? He quickly pulled off his scarf and twined it around her neck. "We'll go out the back where the moonlight's screened by the trees. Hold on to my jacket, okay? I need my hands free, but I don't want you to get lost in the storm."

"Britta could find me," Mara said with a hint of a grin, and for a moment, he saw a flash of the woman he'd been fascinated by back at their Olympia headquarters, the one who was quiet, like him, but brimming with a vibrancy that both interested him and brought back the worst pain he'd ever felt.

He swallowed, gave her his calm, professional cop voice. "If something goes wrong, head downslope and east to my car." He tapped his breast pocket. "The keys are here. Take them and Britta."

She tipped up her chin. "Nothing's going to go wrong. You found me. Now we're all getting out of here together."

He loved the confidence. Amazing considering what she'd endured. Without it, she'd probably not have survived for them to find her.

They retraced their steps to the back. He took a deep breath. "Ready?"

He heard the tiny gulp. "Wait. I almost forgot." She snatched a keychain, the kind with a photo in it, from the slat next to the cardboard box where she must have been sleeping, a memory she would not leave behind.

He understood.

Memories were all he had left too.

Together they climbed onto the windowsill and dropped into the raging storm.

TWO

Mara staggered backward at the blizzard's assault. She clung to Tanner's jacket as best she could while the wind sought to rip them apart. When she slid knee deep into the snow, Britta pulled her back in line.

Everything was a blur, Tanner and Britta's arrival a surreal dream.

You're not alone. Not anymore. The idea was strange and wonderful, and she clung to it, but it did not completely erase the fear. At any moment, a bullet could strike them down, Eli or his man firing from behind one of the thousands of trees that loomed around them.

Just hold on, she told herself. *You made it this far. And now Tanner's here.* The man she'd thought about so often over the last seven months had put his own life at risk to come for her. Mara prayed he and Britta would not pay dearly for their bravery.

Her cheeks burned, flayed by icy flakes. Every step was an enormous effort until she feared she would collapse. After what seemed like forever, Tanner pulled her into the shelter of a fallen tree. The twisted roots cut the wind, a blessed relief. "We can rest a minute."

She couldn't make out his sandy hair or toffee-colored eyes in the gloom, but his voice was ragged with pain.

Pain? She touched his arm. "Are you hurt? Did Eli…"

"Healing from an injury. No biggie."

"What kind of injury?"

"Gunshot."

She swallowed a gasp. "You shouldn't have come."

He cocked his head, lashes glimmering with snow-flakes. "I promised your brother I'd find you. He said I was the man for the job. Not gonna back down from a challenge like that."

The mention of Asher swamped her with conflict-ing emotions. "When I contacted him after it happened, he didn't believe my call or text and we were cut off before I could explain." She'd called him from a pay phone right after fleeing the murder scene, gripping the receiver so hard her fingers cramped.

"Asher, I didn't kill them." She thought she'd heard a sound. He was coming.

"Where are you?"

"Running. Dad's in danger I…"

"Mara, listen to me. You're not acting logically. You have to tell me where you are right now. The evidence is piling up. An anonymous witness says he saw a woman matching your description shoot a young couple. Dan-ica and Colt saw you there and you bolted. Your bracelet was found at the scene. You can't handle this situation by yourself. You need to tell me your location." His words were hard-edged, cold as a mountain winter.

"I…" It had occurred to her then in a flash of nausea that maybe her half brother did not believe her either. Her own flesh and blood…

Tanner's expression was impossible to read in the swirling storm. "He wasn't disputing your innocence. He was trying to tell you to turn yourself in and let the team sort it out."

Would she have gone on and told Asher about Eli if she hadn't noticed the strange man, hired by Eli, approaching the phone booth? If only she'd had her cell she could have sent him the chilling photo Eli had texted her of their father at the care home moments after he'd left the murder scene, but she'd ditched the phone battery since it would give away her location. Asher might have believed her if he'd seen that photo, the clear threat to their father. But she'd bolted from the booth outside that gas station and fled from any chance she had of going back. From there it had become a running for her life scenario. But the team knew the truth now, or most of it anyway. When she got back home she'd spend her every waking moment proving he was the killer.

Might be too late. The thought was bitter. Tanner touched her shoulder and brought her out of the past. "We have to keep moving."

They plowed on, each step a challenge until they reached a flat sweep of snow between the trees, raised on either side to form a natural windbreak. The effort required was exhausting. Her muscles tingled with fatigue. Tanner got out his night vision binoculars. "I don't see any tracks, so they didn't come this way. That's a good sign. My car's just at the edge of the trees over there."

He pointed to a spot that seemed impossibly far away. She tried to keep her voice from revealing her fatigue. "All right."

He pulled a bottle of water from his pack. "Drink?"

"I'm okay." But he held out the bottle anyway, insistent. He was right. She'd been conserving her remaining water so she wouldn't have to go out in the storm to collect more snow to melt in whatever patch of sunlight she could find. Her mouth was parched from breathing hard. Still she felt a flicker of annoyance. *Seven months…*she thought. *I've been surviving on my own and I don't need to be babied now.* It wasn't the time to argue, though. Taking the water, she glugged some down. It restored her, she had to acknowledge.

A moment later they were plunging through the trees again. She realized what he was doing. Though the path straight through the clearing was more direct, it would make them easy pickings for Eli or the other man. The hatred in Eli's tone as he whispered through the door… *let me come in.* If he'd had one more moment… Mara swallowed and tried to keep up with Tanner.

Onward they struggled and she fell twice. Once she scrambled up on her own. Tanner offered his gloved hand the second time with Britta yanking on her jacket sleeve. Cold pummeled her as if she wasn't wearing a coat at all. The extreme chill made her eyes tear until she could no longer see the way forward.

Her lungs burned and the constant sting of driving flakes was disorienting. How much longer could they go on? Had Tanner lost his way? But what other choice did they have? She flailed and pushed until her body screamed for rest.

They made it to a clear path which she realized was some sort of road or trail. Tanner was holding her arm now, half pushing, half guiding her. The light bar of a police car swam into view, the vehicle buried to the top of the tires. She nearly cried in relief. They'd made it. They could drive to safety. Rescue, at last.

"Gonna dig it out. One minute."

He pulled a collapsible shovel from his backpack and within moments he'd cleared a moat around the vehicle. She heard his muttered oath.

"What's wrong?" How could there be anything amiss now that they could escape the murderous cold?

He groaned. "All four tires are flattened, and they bashed in a window and cut the radio." He pointed to the slightly opened hood. "Looks like they took the battery for good measure. They made sure we couldn't drive it out of here."

"No," she whispered as reality sank in. They couldn't continue on in the storm. It would require all their stamina even to make it back to the shelter they'd recently left. Her mind simply wouldn't fasten on any other solutions.

It took all her will to produce words. "We have to go back to the cabin. Barricade ourselves in."

He shook his head. "We won't make it. Storm's not relenting, and we'd be traveling against the wind."

"But we can't stay here. He'll find us."

"Maybe not. Snow covered our tracks. They don't know which way we're headed."

"They'll figure we'd run for the car." She heard the wobble in her own voice. "We can't stay."

"We don't have a choice. No working radio and my portable hasn't worked since the blizzard hit. We have to shelter in the car for at least a few hours. Eli will be battling the same storm we are, and he's not going to be able to come after us until the wind dies down. I can get us some warmth."

"How?" She shook her head. "Too risky."

His hands were on his hips now. "Not arguing right now. There is no other option that doesn't result in us dying from exposure."

"If you want to stay, that's your choice, but I didn't survive seven months on the run to die here. I want to go home." *I want to see my father, my brother.* She turned and started to trudge away; Britta whined high and tense. Tanner caught up and grabbed her forearm.

"Listen to me, please. I know you've been doing it solo all this time, and I can't even imagine how hard that was. But now we have to do this together. We'll shelter in the car. I'll keep watch. If they come for us, I'll see it and we can run. If not, we'll take off before daylight and head back toward the main road where we can spot someone to help us or I can get a cell signal to call the team." She barely felt his gentle squeeze over the growing iciness in her limbs. "Mara, you're right," he said softly. "You've survived too much to let Eli win now."

She was cold, so cold, and weary to the bone. Her brain screamed at her to do something, anything to get out of the frigid onslaught. But getting into that car meant trusting Tanner with her life and she hadn't trusted anyone but herself for seven months, probably longer.

He was still holding her arm, not pulling or squeezing.

"First, tell me one thing. Asher said my father was okay. Truly? Has Eli hurt him?"

"Your father is safe. Asher's made sure of it. He moved him to a safe house."

"Truth?"

Now he squeezed, gently but with conviction. "I would not lie to you."

Every syllable was sincere. "All right," she said through chattering teeth.

Decision made.

She could only pray it was the right one.

Tanner wrenched open the back door and urged Mara and Britta inside before he shut it and made his way to the trunk. His hands were almost useless, but he managed to pull out the bag and slam the trunk shut before bundling himself into the front seat. For a moment, he had to sit motionless, pushing air in and out of his lungs. His fingers burned as he squeezed them into fists to force some circulation. He felt comfortable enough that Eli couldn't approach with the storm raging that he risked activating a flashlight and clumsily duct-taped a tarp over the broken window.

Turning, he found Britta snuggled up tight on Mara's lap. She embraced the dog and they shivered together. He was shivering too. "Here's a blanket." He handed it through an opening in the cage that separated the front seat from the back. "Wrap it around you both."

She did so.

Next he fumbled to activate two chemical hand warmers which she promptly held to her face with her free hand. "I never thought I'd be so grateful for such a tiny bit of heat."

He activated two more. "These can go in your boots."

He thought she might cry. "Do you have any for you?" she said.

"Yes. When I can feel my hands again, I'll install the spare battery I keep in the trunk. Fortunately, they didn't get that."

"A spare battery? You're a wilderness genius."

He laughed. "No. I've just lived places where you don't want to risk being stranded for too long. Dad taught me that trick."

"What if…" She swallowed. "What if the snow keeps falling and we're buried in here?"

"I'll keep an eye on it and go out and shovel if it gets out of hand. Hungry?"

"Do you have food?"

He laughed at the thrilled squeak in her voice. "Hey, this is a full-service rescue operation, ma'am. I never go anywhere without it. We have MREs and such for emergency supplies, but here's something better."

He slid a frozen chocolate bar from his pack. Her expression when she took it sent him hurtling back four years to another face, a precious face who'd smiled just that broadly when he'd accommodated her sweet tooth. His fiancée, Allie, surfaced in his memory, her image clear and sharp.

Allie had accepted the bags of jellybeans he'd brought, with all the black ones removed since she didn't like them. "*Everyone else brings me healthy stuff, but I keep telling them candy is the best medicine.*"

But it hadn't been, nor had the treatments for lymphoma, nor his love and steadfast prayers. Someone told him the wound of losing her would scar over and it wouldn't hurt anymore. After four years the pain had dulled to an ever-present throb, except for odd moments that sucker punched him. Like now, with Mara. For a moment, he couldn't speak for the intense pain that bloomed under his sternum.

"What's wrong?" Mara spoke with the candy bar suspended in her fingers.

"Nothing, aside from the obvious." Britta shot a look at him, head cocked in that comical way. He'd never understood how she sensed his emotions, but she always did, happy, sad or otherwise.

He filled a little bowl with kibble and one with water. "Do you mind putting these on the floor for Britta?"

She did and Britta ate. Tanner was relieved to see his dog behaving normally. Extracting Mara from the cabin had pushed them both to their limits. Mara broke off squares of chocolate and sucked on them, since they were frozen too hard to chew. He did the same. Sweet and bitter as his memories. Maybe that's why he hadn't eaten a lot of chocolate since Allie died.

Installing the spare battery was pure torture but hearing the sound of the heater firing up made it all worthwhile.

"Heat," Mara moaned. "I'll never take it for granted ever again."

The heater had begun to take the edge off the frigid cold when Britta finished her meal and climbed back up into Mara's lap. Tanner twisted sideways in his seat, so he could scan the tree line which was where he suspected an attack would originate if there was one. His revolver was on the seat beside him. Ready. Mara was still shivering, but at least her teeth weren't chattering anymore.

"Just being out of the wind…oh my word. I can't even describe how good it feels."

He concurred, the overworked heater partially restoring circulation to his half-dead limbs. "How did you survive for this long?"

She rested her head on the seat back. "You do what you gotta do, right? I had no other choice. Eli texted me a photo taken with my dad and a message that he'd hurt Dad or Asher if I came forward and I turned myself in. I had to run and buy some time."

Tanner had admired her sharp, fact-based mind and he knew she wouldn't drift aimlessly. "What was your plan?"

"At first, I thought I was going to make my way back, to watch Eli, continue investigating him and find some evidence to prove my own innocence, or maybe the team would get there first." She sighed. "My detecting was what got me on his radar in the first place, why he set up the murders to frame me. I was scouting out a place to host a special birthday party for my father and I looked into one of Stacey Stark's lodges. I saw Eli there, arguing with a man who was carrying heavy crates into the lodge. It was clear they were up to something. I thought I'd do some sleuthing on my own so I was going to take some photos of him, but he spotted me."

Tanner grimaced. "You know it was a PNK9 weapon he used to kill them."

"I don't know how he could have gotten one."

"We're theorizing he knocked out the power to the station, snuck in and appropriated one designated for destruction, which is why it wasn't issued to any particular officer."

"I'm sure that added to the case against me, since I could have gotten access too. I had to run, or at least I thought I did. As long as I could keep him from hurting Asher or my father… I might have been able to elude Eli, but then he sent his guy after me. I couldn't shake them, no matter what I tried or how far I ran."

"Not surprising. Just before I left to find you the team uncovered some info on him. He's a hired gun who goes by the name of Vinny and he's worked for all kinds of bad people, spent time in prison. He's as relentless as they come. His name came up a few weeks ago."

"But how did you find out about the smuggling?"

"Stacey Stark's diaries had been stolen in a different case. We got them back and found the smoking gun— Eli Ballard's motive for killing her. Unfortunately, Jonas just happened to be with her when Eli took action."

Mara hung her head for a moment. "What did Stacey write?"

"That she found out Eli was using the lodges to smuggle and she couldn't abide it. She'd recently become a Christian and it was important to her to do the right thing. She wrote that she was going to confront him— and obviously she did. Scared him enough to silence her."

Mara closed her eyes and said a silent prayer for Stacey and Jonas.

"That was enough to bring him in for questioning," Tanner said, "but he vanished so the chief issued a warrant for his arrest."

"I think about it all, how many times he almost caught me and how close I came to freezing to death and I know I made the wrong choice in taking it on myself to protect Asher and Dad." Her eyes found his.

"I've never been…great at opening up to people, except maybe Willow."

Officer Willow Bates was her only close friend in the unit as far as he could tell. "I understand. Me neither."

She frowned at him. "Really? But you seem so confident, fun loving."

"Sure, but that's all surface stuff. No one really knows me." And he hadn't wanted anyone to after Allie died. Except Mara. Maybe. He shifted. "Anyway, you made your decision and you kept yourself alive. Everyone knows Eli now for what he is."

"I could hardly believe it when I got through to Asher and he told me they were bringing Eli in for questioning. If only I didn't have to hang up so abruptly."

"Asher was pretty desperate to find you right from the start, but he had to work within the system. Eli was crafty for sure. Fooled everyone and covered his tracks. Asher knew Britta and I had the best chance of getting to you, but even so he worried about sending us."

"But you'd been shot recently. Wasn't there anyone else who could come?"

"No way. The job had me and Britta written all over it."

"Why?"

"Because we're the best team in the squad," he bragged, "and I knew you weren't a murderer."

She drew back a fraction and Britta resettled on her lap. "How could you know that?"

Great question. He felt his skin warm. Because he'd admired her no-nonsense style, her quiet, methodical manner, empathized with her struggle to express emotion. "Some things you know in your gut." He was grateful when she didn't press further. A crack from outside made him kill the motor and grab his gun. Britta pushed her squishy jowls against the window.

"Eli?" Mara whispered. Her face was pale as snow in the gloom.

He didn't answer. The storm was buffeting the vehicle with such force he could hear nothing else. Even Britta couldn't warn them of Eli's approach with such a din. The moonlight was completely shrouded by the clouded night sky. "I don't think so. They've got snowmobiles to get around, but they couldn't operate them without lights in this mess. Lie down on the seat with Britta. Try to get some sleep if you can. I'll wake you before dawn."

"But what if it's him?" He heard her gulp.

Then we're going to have ourselves a little meet and greet, he thought, anger balling in his stomach. "I'm keeping watch. Get some sleep. We need to be ready to move out quickly."

It would take all their reserves to complete their escape, especially without a working car.

He peered out into the night, praying that he'd have enough time to fend off an attack if it came.

No, *when* it came.

Eli and Vinny weren't going to back down any more than he was.

Morning would be a long time coming.

Mara woke with a warm ball pressed against her stomach and velvety darkness all around. Blinking awake with a surge of terror, her mind filled in the gaps. She was in a car, Tanner's car, and it was not yet morning, nor could she hear the screeching wind anymore. The interior was freezing cold but tolerable, which meant he must have run the engine periodically.

Britta scrambled out of her lap and onto the seat, leaning over Mara's shoulder to peer out the rear window.

"Tanner?" She struggled to get her stiff body to cooperate. Thanks to Britta's comfort and Tanner's savvy at bringing a spare battery, she was functional. But Tanner must be missing the companionship of his dog.

She twisted to look out the rear window. A shadowy shape… Tanner. The scraping indicated he was moving snow. Squinting, she was able to make out the time on the banged-up wristwatch that used to be her father's… 3:00 a.m. Another interrupted night's rest was nothing new. She'd not slept solidly since her nightmare began.

Britta was happy to climb out with Mara. She realized she could only open the door because Tanner had cleared a spot, the mountain of moved snow a white tower against the night.

He looked up from his shoveling and waved a gloved hand.

"Hi," she whispered, suddenly uncertain. What did you say to a cop who'd babysat you from the front seat of a car all night and was probably half-frozen? Britta greeted him with a happy wag and a gentle pawing before she shook herself and trotted away to find a place to do her business, returning a few moments later.

"Took everything I could from the trunk. We'd better get going."

"Where?"

"The main road is our best chance to signal someone." He handed her a protein bar and a bottle of water and returned to his digging. She hurried off to relieve herself behind a screen of trees, Britta standing near.

There was no escaping the doggie escort. Upon her return, Britta tensed, and squared her body in front of Mara's. Shadows flickered all around her, plops of accumulated snow falling from the branches overhead. Wildly she scanned for Tanner, Britta immovable against her leg, growling low in her throat.

For another long moment she saw nothing, until Tanner appeared. He was moving toward her as fast as he could, turning to use the shovel to collapse the footprints behind him and obliterate hers and Britta's too. She hurried to help him, using a fallen branch to whisk away the marks.

Tanner didn't have to say a word.

They'd been found.

And he was desperately trying to cover their tracks.

THREE

"Gotta move." Tanner pulled at Mara. By then she could hear it for herself, the rumbly engine of a snowmobile. One or two? Her breathing was so ragged she couldn't tell.

Tanner urged her away into the deeper shadows of the trees. "I buried the car again and hopefully concealed our tracks enough. They'll either assume we didn't make it to the vehicle or we're still inside. Hopefully it will slow them down anyway."

"Shouldn't we stay? Try and capture them?" *End this thing once and for all?*

"Too risky. One of them will approach and stage the other as backup. I won't be able to cover them both at once."

That was Eli. Relentless, but cautious, never one to risk his own safety without an escape plan. They moved slowly and carefully away from the buried vehicle. Tanner kept them to the densely spaced pines. It was slow going, their boots punching through the hard crust and miring them in the fluff underneath. Only Britta seemed unfazed by the effort, her feet protected in dog-sized snow boots. Behind the shelter of a massive trunk, he stopped.

"Let's rest a minute." His voice was barely above a murmur. "Don't want to sweat right now. It will accelerate hypothermia."

"You know a lot about this survival stuff?" she whispered back.

"Born and raised in Alaska. We know how to do winters."

She hadn't known that about him. Mara was not the nosy type. As a matter of fact she could be acquainted with people for the longest time without ever really delving into their personal lives since she didn't want them doing the same with hers. Yet she'd found Tanner Ford interesting.

Not the time, nor the place. They focused on catching their breath. The pause allowed them to better hear the sound of a revving engine. She tensed. Tanner put a finger to his lips, pulled out binoculars and focused the lenses.

"It's Vinny. He's going to dig out the car so they must not have seen our tracks. Excellent. That will buy us minutes."

Minutes maybe, but Eli, intelligent and ruthless, would not be tricked by the ruse for long. He was watching, waiting, keeping himself safe from risk, using Vinny to do the dirty work. Like he'd appropriated Stacey Stark's cabins to move his stolen guns and merchandise, and he'd used Mara's own father to threaten her when she'd begun to suspect him.

Dad... She visualized again her father's dazed expression, a byproduct of the Alzheimer's which was eating away his mind. The photo in her keychain was one of the two of them, her dad in his favorite yellow sweater. The image captured his smile, now almost permanently vanished from his expression. What she'd give to see him grin again. The familiar prickle of fear tightened her chest. She didn't know why the Lord had allowed her dad to succumb to the terrible disease when he'd finally asked forgiveness for being unfaithful to Asher's mother. The wounds from his infidelity ran deep, but they were making strides. With her father's blessing, she'd reached out to her half brother, even applied to the PNK9 team in the hopes of deepening their relationship while she pursued her professional goals. Progress, she'd thought, until things had spiraled out of control.

But Tanner was here now, which confirmed that God hadn't forgotten her. And her father was okay, she told herself sternly. And Eli would be caught and tossed in jail where he belonged. If only they could escape.

The engine noise grew louder. It felt as though the trees had eyes, staring, tracking their every labored step. Tanner gave Britta the silent command and the dog sat alert, motionless, watching for the next instruction.

The snowmobile rumbled closer to their hiding spot, so close she could feel the vibration under her feet. Eli spoke. She jumped but managed to keep from making any noise. He must be talking on a phone or radio.

"What?" Eli barked, his tone so different from the friendly smooth talker who was a buddy to one and all.

There was a crackle of static and Vinny replied. "No one in the car. Maybe they didn't come back for it."

"Where else could they go to shelter? The storm

was ferocious and there's another front coming in by nightfall."

"They're probably dead, buried in the snow somewhere."

"I'm not going to be satisfied until I see their bodies, especially hers. She's the only eyewitness that can put me there at the scene of the murders. If she's dead, their case may be too."

"They've still got you for the smuggling."

"I'll wriggle out of it. I'm smarter than they are."

"But she's not alone now. Not a good idea to kill a cop. And the dog counts as a cop too. There's no going back once you pull the trigger."

"No choice. I can pull off Mr. Misunderstood to a jury about the smuggling, but if she takes the stand and convinces them I killed Stacey and Jonas... They always believe the woman. We'll kill them and bury them somewhere where they'll never be found."

"It's your dime," Vinny said.

"Yes, it is. So get going. Wind's picking up, and I want to get back to our camper before my feet are frostbitten. Who would ever want to live in the middle of all this snow?"

Mara realized she was biting her lip to keep from screaming as Eli discussed their murders not five feet from her hiding place. As if they weren't two living, breathing human beings. As a crime tech she was accustomed to heinous killings, but she'd never been so exposed to the cold-blooded planning of one.

The motor thrummed and grew fainter as Eli drove off.

Tanner blew out a breath. "Close shave. Are you okay?"

She nodded furiously, but tears dimmed her vision anyway. "Not every day you hear someone plotting your death." She tried to make it sound casual, but her voice wobbled.

Tanner wrapped an arm around her shoulders and drew her closer. His lips brushed her ear. "You're not alone anymore, Mara. He's not gonna win. Britta and I are here to make sure."

She could not speak around the lump in her throat. After countless days of solitude, it felt wonderful to have Tanner touching her, lifting a corner of the darkness that had cloaked her for months. She'd liked him from the first day she'd started on the job, but as with all of her other coworkers she'd kept herself distant, aloof, all business but now here he was…up close and personal.

She tried to shake away the emotion. He detached himself from her, brushing the snow from his pants and rising as if the touch hadn't meant to him what it had to her.

Distant, aloof, all business.

This was no different than her work behavior, and she'd better follow her own rules. She'd gotten what she'd asked for by being rescued and that was the only important aspect of her relations with Tanner, even if her heart seemed to be wanting more.

Survival, she told herself.

That was all she needed. The emotional stuff could be sorted out later.

"The road's about three miles that way." Tanner pointed in the direction Eli had taken.

Her eyes widened. "But…"

"It's our best shot at getting help."

She understood.

Probably their only shot.

Eli or no Eli, they had no other choice.

They were headed straight into the lion's mouth.

Tanner felt the cold stealing away his strength. Mara was already lagging behind and Britta too, had slowed, ice coating her harness. "Only a little longer to the road," he encouraged.

Mara nodded and he took her hand. Together they struggled through waist-high drifts. He didn't bother to check his watch, but he figured it was close to 5:00 a.m. They'd survived until morning.

Thank you, God, he silently prayed.

If he was alone, he'd time out the route in ruthless intervals. Move for fifteen minutes, rest for five. It was how he lived his day-to-day, one task to the next, not allowing too much time in between for thought or painful memories. He knew God, believed Him, but he simply could not rest in Him, or anyone or anything.

Mara floundered, sinking knee-level in the snow. He hauled her out, and she leaned on him, panting. She needed rest soon. All three of them did. The roadway was one more pitched slope away. After she caught her breath, they struggled on. The last ten steps were pure agony, but finally they climbed up onto the flat stretch of glistening white.

He recognized the problem immediately, heart sinking.

"The snow's deep," she said as she took in their surroundings. "It hasn't been plowed."

There was no tiptoeing around the grim facts. "Road's closed."

"No, it can't be." Mara shook her head in disbelief. "Surely they'll clear it." An edge of desperation crept into her voice. "Someone will come."

He glanced at the sky which should be proclaiming the morning, but was lightening only enough to illuminate another thick wall of clouds. He wished he didn't have to tell her, not after all she'd suffered already, but he wouldn't try to sugarcoat things. She'd be strong, he knew. "Mara, I heard a guy talking about the possibility when I last refueled. This isn't a main road, more of a truck stopover than a thoroughfare." He took a breath. "They said the plows and snow movers would be diverted to the highway if necessary." The highway...that was clear on the other side of the mountain.

The silver light caught the bleakness in her eyes which he knew from their past working together in Olympia were the iridescent green of the northern lights.

"No help?" she said weakly. "We'll have to hike to the highway?"

"That's not an option."

"What do you mean?"

"It's not feasible with a second storm front coming. We'd never make it."

"Then what?"

Then what? his mind echoed. *You are responsible for two other lives here. Figure it out, Ford.* "About a half mile up the road is a gas station with a mini-mart–type thing. There might be someone there still, or at least a way I can break in and we can shelter in place, try for a phone signal."

soul-sucking cold. Forcing a confidence he did not feel, he whacked on the door. "Hey," he yelled. "Anybody in there?"

He heard nothing and the door was securely locked when he jiggled it. The windows were barred. What was plan B? He had a small collapsible tent in his backpack, but the temperature was dropping and there was barely a hint of the rising sun behind the clouds. In his peripheral vision he could not miss the way Mara slumped shivering, head down. She had likely had no solid rest or food for ages. What could he do? His mind pinwheeled from one useless notion to the next.

Britta sat up straighter, head cocked.

She'd heard movement from the interior. He blinked to make sure he wasn't seeing things before he pounded again. "Anyone inside? We need help."

After what seemed like an eternity, a small, balding man opened the door a crack. Tanner felt like shouting his joy to the clouds.

The man looked out, anxious eyes with puffy bags underneath. "We're closed."

Tanner twitched in surprise. "Sir, I'm Officer Tanner Ford of the Pacific Northwest K-9 Unit, and I have a dog and a woman with me. This is an emergency. We need shelter."

"I'm sorry. I can't help you."

Tanner was almost too incredulous to react, but he stuck his boot in the door and pulled his badge from under his jacket in case the man thought he was lying. "Yes you can." *And you will.* "All you have to do is let us in, sir. Like I said, I'm law enforcement and we need a place to shelter. We won't cause you any trouble, but this is a life or death matter and I need you to comply."

He saw the man visibly gulp. Why was he so scared? Did Tanner look that intimidating? He shoved the badge closer. "Proof that I am who I say I am. You've got to let us in."

After a charged moment, he stepped back and opened the door. Mara mumbled her heartfelt thanks and Britta accompanied her inside.

"Thank you," Tanner added as they staggered into the mini-mart area. The refrigerated cases were dark and the lingering scent of stale coffee made his mouth water. "What's your name, sir?"

"Howard Brown." He jabbed a finger toward a narrow hallway. "There's a break room and a bathroom. You can stay in there until you warm up."

"Do you have phone service? Electricity?" he pressed.

"No. No one does. I live about ten miles from here, but I came in to lock up the place and my car died. No matter. I got what I need here until my wife comes." His eyes slid to Mara and then quickly away. "I'll get you some food."

Little hairs on Tanner's arms lifted. Something wasn't right, but what choice did they have? Certain death outside. They found the break room which was cold, but not intolerable. After they both used the miniscule bathroom, they settled into the two chairs at the scarred table. There was no Wi-Fi signal or phone connection. Britta nosed around the space, sniffing the boxes labeled toilet paper and rubber gloves, the tiny wastebasket.

Howard opened the door carrying two chipped mugs with tea bags in them.

Mara clutched the warm drink. "Thank you so much, Howard."

Again he gave her that look, half curious, half sorrowful. Tanner waited for him to ask questions. Who wouldn't when a couple of desperate characters showed up at his doorstep? How had they gotten stranded? Where was his vehicle? But Howard simply dropped two granola bars and a box of dog biscuits on the table, turned and left, closing the door behind him.

Tanner stared at the door.

"He's a little…odd," Mara said.

"Odd doesn't quite cover it."

She tore open the granola bar and chewed a bite, eyes rolling. "And I don't even like raisins, but this tastes amazing."

He stuffed his into his pocket and opened the sealed box of dog treats. "At least he's a dog lover."

Britta gulped up the treats, but soon went back to her sniffing.

"Why was Howard so reluctant to let us in?"

"Could be he's been robbed before. Didn't trust that I was actually a cop."

Britta shook her floppy ears. Staring into Tanner's eyes, she sat stiffly next to the trash can. Tanner's stomach contracted.

"What's she trying to tell you?" Mara held the warm mug tight to her chest.

Tanner walked over and peered into the trash can. Nothing much in there, but Britta had a nose for scent. He pulled out a balled-up paper, wondering. Why was Britta reacting? She'd been tuned to one of two scents, Mara's…and Eli's.

He smoothed out the crumpled ball.

"What is it?" Mara asked.

Time ticked slowly to a stop. He held up the creased paper, a photocopy of her smiling face from the department website. Mara Gilmore, crime scene tech.

She stared. "How...why is that in the trash can?"

"Eli was here. He's working with Howard." Tanner was already at the door, yanking at the knob.

It was locked.

Mara's eyes met his.

They'd walked right into a trap.

FOUR

Mara winced as Tanner rammed his shoulder into the door. No good. The wood was as solid as the lock. She attempted to calm Britta who was whining, ears flapping as she tried to understand what was upsetting her master. She stroked the dog's thick neck, feeling every muscle in the sleek body as tense as her own. Howard had locked them in and sold them out to Eli. For money? Out of fear? Didn't matter much.

Tanner tried again, aiming his boot at the spot below the door handle. His force was tremendous, but again, there was no sign it was helping. They were trapped inside like fish waiting to be harpooned.

Mara thought Tanner was going to kick at the door once more but instead he ran to the back of the room and tossed aside some stacked boxes. She'd overlooked the edge of an exit peeking above the towering pile, but he hadn't. Her pulse raced. A second door, another chance.

She bolted to help him, still trying to make their situation real in her mind. She'd known there was something off about Howard, but they'd been so cold, so desperate, there had been no other choice but to accept his help. The cartons fell into untidy piles around them as they burrowed their way to the door.

Tanner tried the handle. Mara held her breath.

It turned and he shoved hard to open it. Elation filled her body for a couple of seconds until she realized there was another barrier. Freezing air blasted them both through a barred security panel fixed over the exit door. They both pushed at it, shoving hard at the iron rods.

Tanner pressed his face to the cold metal and thrust his hand through, groping around. "It's padlocked from the outside with a chain. Good old Harold probably figured it'd be safe from vandals until he could get back here." The chain clanged as he tugged at it with no success.

Mara felt like screaming. Instead she ran back to the other door and pressed her ear close. "I can hear talking, more than one person but I can't be sure." Her heart trip hammered. "They're coming closer."

Tanner's gaze raked the room, and he unsnapped his holster. "Gonna have to make a stand here." The light caught his eyes, the shimmer of caramel, the glimmer of an apology. "I'm sorry, Mara. This isn't much of a rescue."

"You don't have anything to be sorry about." But *she* did. He'd come for her, sent by her half brother, Asher, because she'd not trusted the process, figured she'd be better off without her team. Brought him and Britta into a death trap to rescue her. Tanner Ford and his exceptional dog did not deserve to die because of her choices.

It was suddenly hard to swallow. Her brain refused to stop looking for a way out, but now she could hear the faint sound of approaching footsteps. "They're coming."

He upended the table and urged her behind it.

She stood her ground. "No. It's going to take us both to have any chance."

His eyes narrowed. "There will be shooting, Mara. I'll try to draw them away as much as I can. If you get a chance, run out the door." He pushed his backpack at her. "Take this and hide. There's food for Britta too."

She shook her head. "No heroics. Two have a better chance than one, especially if Vinny is with Eli."

His jaw tensed. "This isn't heroism—it's my job. I'm a cop. I'm going to do what I'm trained to."

Her chin went up. "And I've been surviving these two clowns for seven months so I'm going to do what *I've* been training for." She crouched next to the table and grabbed up a chair, wielding it like a lion tamer. "When they come close enough, whammo." *If the bullets didn't get her first.*

The sliver of a smile crossed his mouth. With one hand he reached down to caress Britta's ears. The gesture said it all. Tanner loved his dog every bit as deeply as Britta loved him back. The animal would likely not survive either. Her eyes went watery. This couldn't be happening. It was not possible it would all end here.

He pointed behind the table. "Britta, wait."

Pain rippled Tanner's face. Pain and fear ricocheted in her chest as the dog sidled around her and edged behind the table. The voices were louder now, the back and forth rhythm indicating an argument.

Tanner stepped to the side of the door and drew his revolver.

Her fingers were clammy on the chair legs, breath coming in spurts. Would Eli and Vince enter firing? Send

Howard in first to create a distraction? Maybe Howard would be armed too. Three of them with one goal. Murder. Blood pounded in her throat.

Britta stood on her rear paws, popped her head over the edge of the table and barked a moment before the chain on the rear door rattled. She gasped. Trying to understand. Someone was at the back exit? Eli must've sent Vinny around.

The noise jerked Tanner's attention and he swiveled his revolver to the exit. A face showed between the security bars, a wisp of long gray hair framing wrinkled cheeks.

Now she was completely confused. *Who in the world...?*

A pair of bolt cutters intruded on the space.

"Hurry," a female voice urged. With a clack, the chain was cut loose, the barred door opening to reveal a short woman bundled in a ski jacket, hat and muffler. "Come quick. We only have a few minutes."

Tanner looked at Mara, gun still aimed at the newcomer. He knew what she did. Stranger or not, this was their one and only chance of escape. "Follow," he told Britta who scrambled from behind the table and jogged after the woman who was hurrying into the swirling snowflakes. Tanner grabbed his pack and Mara hers and they ran after the lady who didn't bother to lock the door. Their rescuer hurried away from the gas station proper toward a storage shed behind the property. Mara couldn't hear anything from the building they'd just vacated so she had no idea if Eli had discovered they'd escaped.

And what about Vinny? Had they split up? Was he

tracking them even now? The wind was blowing so hard it drove horizontally into her, stinging like the lash of a whip. The woman tossed the bolt cutters on the ground. There was no choice but to follow her across the piled snow and into the shed. She wrestled the door closed and turned to face them.

"I'm Alice. Married to Howard."

Mara tried to hide her fear. Was this part of some other plan Howard was involved in?

"My husband isn't a bad man."

"He told Eli Ballard where to find us," Tanner said. "And Eli is a murderer. That makes your husband a criminal too."

Her mouth tightened. "No. Howard made a bad decision that he regrets. He's been knocked down by life too many times and it washed away some of his grit, that's all. When those two thugs came and offered him money to rat you two out, he took it. I didn't find out about it until he finally admitted as much when I showed up a few minutes ago to find out why he hadn't arrived home. I'm here to get him out of his mess by helping you two get away."

She moved to the corner of the shed and shoved aside a trapdoor in the floor. It opened with a toe-curling squeal. From her pocket she pulled a key attached to a small chain. "This shaft will take you underground to a utility tunnel. After that, follow the fire trail a mile south and you'll come to a trailer. Belonged to my uncle. He died and I was going to put it up for sale. I was working on packing things up when the weather turned bad. Use whatever you need."

Tanner took the key and finally interrupted. "Ma'am,

if all this is true, you're putting yourself in danger by helping us. I can't leave you and your husband…"

She waved him off. "I hope it's going to look like you two found the bolt cutters in the break room and managed to escape by yourselves. I'm going to sneak out of here and double back and act as if I just drove up so they won't know about my involvement. Snow's falling and the wind's vicious so our tracks will be harder to spot. If everything works out, we'll be gone in my truck before they figure it out."

"They're dangerous men," Mara said. "They might hurt your husband when they find us gone."

She shook her head. "By all appearances, he cooperated. He's more likely to pay the price if you two get us involved in a gun battle on the premises."

"I…" Tanner started.

She snatched a rusty kerosene lantern and a box of matches from the shelf and thrust them at Mara. "I don't have time to argue the point. Go. Please. I'll call the police and tell them your location as soon as I can get a line out."

Tanner nodded. "All right." He holstered his gun and offered his palm. "You saved our lives, ma'am."

She shook and grinned. "Retired army. 'This we'll defend' is our motto. Right now I'm choosing to defend you and my husband as best I can. Get going, so it wasn't all for nothing."

Mara caught the woman's eye. "Thank you."

She shrugged. "My Howard's a good man, deep down. Just remember that, okay? And honestly you two are going to have an uphill battle, my help aside. Those men aren't going to stop and even if I get through to the cops, you'll be on your own until the storm system passes. It's horrible weather unlike anything I can remember." She snatched a thick moving blanket from the pile. "Take this too. It'll be freezing down there."

A shout came from the direction of the gas station. "Please," she urged. "We're out of time. I'll move some boxes over the trapdoor to add to the ruse before I sneak out and lock the shed from the outside, but you gotta go *now*."

Tanner picked Britta up and draped her over his shoulders. Britta took the opportunity to slop a tongue over his ear. Mara turned around, tossed the blanket down and then descended the first few steps of the worn wooden ladder. Alice gave her a thumbs-up. The woman's determined expression reminded her of Willow, her only friend on the PNK9 team. Recrimination left a bitter taste in her mouth. Why hadn't she worked harder to get to know the others? Why was there always the thinnest layer of glass between her and the people around? But not with Willow. God had somehow prompted her to make a connection with her gutsy, honest and compassionate friend. Mara wondered if she'd ever see her again.

The wooden ladder creaked. And her half brother, Asher? All she'd wanted for years was to form a bond with him, her only sibling. She had a chance, now that he knew for certain she was innocent of murder. A bubble of resentment formed in her stomach. He should have believed her from the first, trusted her. But why would he when they hardly knew each other and their father had hurt Asher so deeply? Abandoned Asher and his mom to start a new family? A wound like that ran deep.

Would she live long enough to start fresh with her brother?

Only if Alice's brave ruse worked.

With each rung the cold intensified. Swallowing hard, she forced herself to descend into the darkness.

Tanner followed Mara down. Britta's weight on his shoulders was somehow comforting, bringing him to earth mentally as she always did no matter what the circumstances. Even when he wasn't sure what he was feeling, Britta seemed to know. Right now his body was still coursing with adrenalin, head spinning at Howard's betrayal and their unexpected rescue. Two more civilians had stepped into the line of fire. He felt somewhat certain that Eli would not risk piling up bodies that might attract more attention, but there was no way to be certain. He whispered a prayer that Alice and Howard would escape unharmed.

Thank you, Alice. The woman had stuck her neck out to save two strangers. She was a strong woman, like the one who was currently easing her way down the ladder below him. He reached up and pulled the trapdoor closed. It banged down, sending a drift of dust settling into his ski cap and hair and snuffing out the light. The tunnel smelled of mold, with a slight tang of something muskier. Nothing feral, he hoped. Britta sneezed, spraying his cheek with dog slobber.

"You all right?" he called down to Mara.

"Yes. Almost to the bottom."

His numbed hands felt flabby against the wood, but gloves would hamper his grip even more and he needed every bit of finger strength. The ladder creaked and groaned under him. Three more steps and his left boot went clear through an aged rung, almost flinging Britta loose. Mara cried out, but he clutched Britta with his free hand and she curled tightly around his neck to keep her balance. They'd practiced this very maneuver, but they'd not actually tried it out while climbing down a ladder. She licked the top of his head, encouraging him.

"That was scary." Her voice sounded shaky.

"Yeah. I'll try not to repeat the performance."

He eased down the rungs more carefully. A light flared below. She'd reached the bottom and got the lantern working. The final twenty rungs seemed impossibly long. When his boots touched ground, he lowered Britta and she started to work her curious nose around the space. Mara held up the light. They were in a tunnel, earthen walls supported by old beams he hoped were more intact than the ladder.

He flicked on a flashlight to supplement the lantern. Mara's face was gilded by the glow, dark hair blending with the gloom. Her teeth chattered, though she appeared to be gripping her jaw tight to prevent it.

"Wrap the blanket around yourself."

"I thought maybe you or Britta might need it."

He chuckled. Like he would use the blanket himself instead of insisting she take it. "No, ma'am. Wrap up and let's get out of here before Eli catches on." He could be figuring out their trick at that very moment.

The tunnel stretched out ahead of them, the floor littered in some places with small rocks. He was uncomfortably cold, but it was vastly better than suffering in the blasting maelstrom outside. Discomfort was something a person could learn to live with, he'd discovered. Alice's plan was a clever one. It was possible Eli wouldn't think to investigate the locked shed and if he did, he might not discover the hidden trapdoor.

Doubt winnowed into his thoughts. Eli was smart. He'd run a gun smuggling operation out of Stacey Stark's lodges, after all, dated PNK9 cop Ruby Orton even, and his cohort was an experienced killer. Some of Mara, Tanner and Britta's tracks from the gas station to the shed might have survived the snowstorm long enough to give them away. Or might he have forced Alice to tell the truth? Urged on by his nerves, he set a brisk pace.

Mara kept up at his side, stepping around rocks and over piles of animal droppings. The heavy blanket swaddled her from neck to knees. "Do you think Alice and Howard will be okay?"

"Best-case scenario is they'll get away from here as quick as they can while Eli is out scouring the woods for us."

She was silent. He knew she didn't underestimate Eli either. She'd been his target long enough not to make that mistake. Good old Eli, a handsome genial friend to all, hiding his killer instincts underneath the charming facade.

Her hand was steady as she held the lantern, and he was happy to see she was warming up. The fringe of hair peeking from beneath her pom-pom hat gave her an elfin look, and he wished he could take a picture to capture the mixture of femininity and undeniable grit. He found her exciting, interesting. *Knock it off.* The spark he'd felt for her since the day they'd met at

PKN9 headquarters was just fondness, like he felt for his younger sister Livvy or another close pal.

Who was he kidding? He hadn't had a close pal since Allie died, and he strove to keep it that way. For some reason, as he trucked along the tunnel with Mara, their age difference didn't even feel like a blip on the radar. He wanted to watch her, listen to her talk, hear her thoughts on anything and everything. His heart beat with unusual quickness. It struck fear into his psyche, that spark he felt. Not again, not ever again.

Just keep the conversation moving. Easy and charming and don't make it anything more than it is. Not a problem, he was a master at surface level relationships. "How did you do it, Mara? Survive on your own for so long? It's one thing to go off grid, but another when an entire law enforcement unit is chasing you down."

"And two killers, don't forget." He liked the hint of pride in her voice. Her exhale turned to visible steam in the lantern light. "Sheer determination, I think. My father taught me how to play chess. I can still hear him saying, 'Marbles, chess is a battle played out on a board.'" She rolled her eyes. "You know, I used to detest that nickname when I was a teen, but now, I'd give my right arm to hear him call me that." He heard her swallow.

He knew from Asher that their father was losing himself to Alzheimer's in what had to be a long and agonizing goodbye for Mara. His instinct was to offer comfort. Her demeanor told him otherwise.

She tightened the blanket around her shoulders. "Anyway, I decided I was going to do whatever I had to do to keep Eli from winning, and wage that battle in my own way. I was going to protect Asher and Dad and find evidence against Eli." She grinned. "But thanks for doing that last part for me…even though it took you all seven months."

Again the cheeky bravado. He laughed. "You've done incredibly well to outwit him and us, for that matter. We never even came close to tracking you." He hoped he hadn't sounded too admiring. Casual and light, remember?

She shrugged. "To be fair, I didn't make much progress at all digging up proof. I was too busy trying to survive."

"What did you do for money? The unit tracked your credit cards and ATM, of course, but there was no activity after that first withdrawal."

She quirked a smile at him. "Tricky, right? I went to an out-of-the-way ATM wearing a hat and glasses and withdrew as much cash as I could before I left Olympia. When it ran low, I worked some shifts at out-of-the-way diners as I moved from town to town, and let me tell you I learned how to bus a table in a heartbeat. I even earned some money shoveling snow a time or two. Talk about backbreaking. I think I still have the blisters."

"How'd you move around?"

"I knew you could track my cell, so I took the battery out. Walked or hitchhiked, to avoid the public cameras everywhere. I kept my hair covered by a cap all the time. Tossed the blue jacket and bought this one at a thrift shop the first possible moment. I figured the best way to win the battle was to keep moving all night and during the day I stayed in cheap hotels mostly until Eli got close or my money ran low. Sunday was my favorite day."

"Why's that?"

Her smile was dreamy or maybe it was merely a trick of the lantern light. "I found a few churches with coffee and snacks."

She drew out the word *snacks* as if she was discussing a profound revelation. "Bagels and cream cheese, homemade cookies and sometimes donuts, if you can believe it. I would sit way in the back and listen to the sermons, warm up, keep my eyes on the door in case Eli tracked me and scoot out before the end of the service. Most congregations never even realized I was there."

He chuckled.

"The food was a blessing, but more than that, I heard a lot of different preachers and they all reminded me that no matter what happened, God had the final word. It kept me going." She gave him the side-eye. "Are you a churchgoer, Tanner?"

God has the final word. Wait on the Lord and He will give you courage and healing. How often had he heard the same messages? And he believed it, yet he'd stopped going to church after Allie died. He'd grown tired of waiting, suffering, summoning up the courage to face people. "I…was."

"But you gave it up?"

He shrugged. "I guess I did."

She didn't ask, but he knew she was waiting for him to explain. "I uh, lost someone I cared about, and everyone wanted to console me. I didn't want to accept comfort from any of them. It hurt too much."

Gently she touched his forearm. "I understand." She sighed. "I guess what's come home to me lately is that I walked, no flat out ran, from people who God had positioned to help me. He must have just smacked His head at my denseness."

He suddenly remembered what his mother used to say when he retreated into his customary silent manner as a teen. "*We're commanded to love one another and when you don't allow people to do that, you rob them of a blessing.*"

He'd sure tried to bless Allie with everything in him and after her death he'd become unable to receive love in return. Funny how he'd never really considered that blessings were a boon to the giver as well as the receiver. But this wasn't a conversation he wanted to have…not with Mara. "Anyway, you should win the fugitive of the year award." He got what he wanted. Her hand fell away from his arm and the distance between them reinstated their relationship, chums, colleagues, joined together on a mission. A whisper of regret circled through him.

Mara continued her story. "Eli got close a few times so I knew I needed to head farther afield, away from Olympia, vanish into a more rural area. There's a campground near Mount Rainier where my dad used to take me. Always loved it as a kid, like being on a different planet away from civilization. That's where I hinted to Asher I'd be." She groaned. "It's way more fun when you're on vacation instead of running for your life. I made it there, but I only stayed for a few hours. Eli caught up, and I had to bolt. I've been bouncing from campground to campground until I stumbled on that empty cabin where you and Britta found me."

He chuckled and pulled a mitten from his pocket. "Britta did the finding. We used this as a scent article. You dropped it."

She laughed, the sound bouncing off the tunnel walls. "You can totally outwit people, but you can't fool a dog."

"That's for sure, but it was slow going when the blizzard landed. It would have been way easier in the summer."

She rolled her eyes. "Tell me about it. That totally made things ten times harder. The storm systems arrived about the same time I did. I might have changed my mind and called to turn myself in, but I had no way to contact anyone. I called Asher from a payphone and when I checked in with Willow, it was because I begged a lady in the grocery store to allow me to borrow her phone."

He could only marvel at her ingenuity. Clever woman.

The lamplight revealed a door twenty feet ahead of them. Britta bounded ahead to give it a once-over.

"Looks like we made it to the exit." He was glad to end the line of conversation they'd had going. He'd begun to enjoy the sound of her voice way more than he should have, the way it rose and fell like the breeze coming over the mountains.

She held the light so he could see the rusted panel. The wind outside pummeled the door like fists. Again his mind started churning up thoughts. Mara picked up on his hesitation.

"You're thinking this might not be an escape after all. Eli could be waiting. He could have decided trapping us here was a perfect way to kill us. Far away from a building. Alice and Howard not around to be witnesses."

He tried not to let his concern show, but she'd gotten every point that had been worrying him. She was a fellow investigator, after all, though her business was crime scenes, not law enforcement. Her job, dusting for fingerprints, searching for evidence and collecting samples all required thinking out of the box so she wouldn't miss anything.

Was the metal door an escape or a shield? Normally Britta could detect Eli's presence with the blizzard howling around them...

"Seems like we have two choices here. Go out or return via the tunnel to the shed. Either way Eli could be there waiting, or Vinny or both of them."

She chewed her lip in thought. "There's a third choice. Stay here for a while."

He had to hold back an uncomfortable squirm. "Like being a bug trapped in a bottle."

"I agree." She gazed into the darkness in the direction of the ladder and then looked straight at him. "I trust Alice. She put her life on the line to help us. If she thinks we can get to the trailer, I say we go for it."

"Confident, are you?"

"God didn't bring me this far for it all to end here."

He wanted to feel that same surety, but God had ended things for Allie after he'd been so certain, so completely confident that she would live. But this wasn't then. Mara was willing to risk going forward and he intended to be right there with her until the moment he delivered her safely back to Olympia. He'd promised Asher, and himself.

He pulled his knit cap lower on his forehead and put one palm on the door. "Flank," he said to Britta, who took up a position at his side. She showed no sign that she'd picked up the scent of danger.

Mara tucked the blanket under her arm, the lantern

in one hand, the other palm held up as if she was expecting a blow.

Here goes nothing, he thought as he eased the door open.

FIVE

Mara's pulse galloped as the blast of cold knocked her back. Britta flattened her stocky frame against the onslaught.

Tanner eyed Britta carefully, but she didn't seem to be alerting on any malicious presence. Mara couldn't see how any creature, even the incredible boxer, could detect a human over the howling din. Maybe she couldn't. They might be walking right into an execution.

Throat dry, she stayed close to Tanner. They pushed out, Tanner, one step ahead, gun in his gloved hand. He shoved a rock in the tunnel door to keep it from closing completely in case it automatically locked from the outside. A last-ditch fail-safe if they could not find the trailer. It would also show Eli their escape route if he tracked them this far.

Between a rock and a hard place, she thought grimly. She'd folded the blanket in a tight roll and gripped it under her arm to keep her hands free. For what? To fight off a bullet from Eli? In an instant, every thought and fear in her mind was sucked away save for the overwhelming sense that her body was freezing one cell at a time.

All around was a stinging machine gun spray of snowflakes barreling at them. In a matter of moments, she'd completely lost her sense of direction.

Tanner pulled her close, tugged the blanket from under her arm and wrapped it around her. Flakes powdered his lashes. "Storm's picked up. I can't find a trail."

Lost, her brain screamed. In these conditions it would mean certain death. She spun around, but she could no longer see the tunnel behind them. As her terror edged toward despair, she saw Tanner reach into his pocket and pull out Alice's key. He offered Britta a sniff. Mara felt a prick of hope. Alice had said she had been at her uncle's recently, packing. Her scent would be on both the key and the trailer. Their fate rested on Britta's furry shoulders, or maybe on her coal-black nose.

Britta's nostrils quivered as she inhaled the scent. Tail erect, she surged ahead. Tanner holstered his weapon, took Mara's hand and they followed. In near whiteout conditions, bent almost double, they pushed on one step at a time, past sculpted mounds of snow that might have been shrubs, trees or piles of rock. She could no longer feel Tanner's hand in hers though she wore the lined gloves he'd pulled from his backpack and insisted she put on. Dizzy, freezing, disoriented, she struggled on, able only to spot glimpses of Britta.

The moments passed in slow motion with no sign of a trailer or any other shelter that might protect them. Had they been walking for five minutes? Fifteen? The storm only intensified as they moved on. Another ten minutes? Twenty? Her eyes leaked moisture which froze stiff on her cheeks until she could not even make out Britta's dark sides anymore. Had the dog gotten sucked up in the howling storm? Her heart lurched. Poor, brave Britta who should be back in Olympia sleeping in her cozy bed.

They could not continue much longer, but would they even have the strength to return to the tunnel? She'd been wrong to advise them to leave it. Wrong about it all and now it was time for them all to pay for her mistake. "Tanner…"

Had she actually produced a sound? It was like shouting in the wash of a jet engine. She had to try again, to say they needed to return to the tunnel and take their chances with Eli before it was too late. But Tanner was stopped, staying something to her. She couldn't hear a syllable of it.

He leaned so close his cold lips brushed her cheek. She made out the last word. "…here."

Here? Where?

He took her arm and half dragged her underneath the trees. Weren't they heading away from the trail? Thanks to the whiteout, she no longer had any idea where the gas station was, the trail, the tunnel. The landscape might as well have been on some other planet. Britta kept vanishing in the deep snow, then popping up as she bounced herself free. There was no doubt she was struggling.

Tanner shouted something again, which she did not hear. Too numb to think, she allowed him to tow her along. It was all a disorienting kaleidoscope, and she was not sure she was even still on her feet, until he stopped.

"Wait here."

She blinked hard, standing in a stupor as he waded

through a deep hollow, the snow clear to his waist. Her eyes burned and she had a hard time forcing them to blink. Suddenly, he yanked open a door seemingly in the middle of a snowbank. She must be hallucinating, she thought as she swiped the ice from her brows. Her brain slowly accepted what her eyes were reporting. Not a snowbank, her mind sang. A snow-covered structure, a narrow door with a silver handle, the door to a white trailer almost halfway swallowed up.

In disbelief, she watched Britta climb up with help from Tanner and then he'd returned to her, seized her waist and hoisted her uncooperative body over his shoulder, carrying her to the trailer steps. When he set her down, her legs were so wooden she could not crawl up so he lifted her in, joining her after a moment. He slammed the door shut against the raging storm.

Inside? They'd found shelter? Everything was an unrecognizable blur. Tanner pushed her to a bench seat bordering a tiny kitchen table, sat down beside her and called Britta to him. When the dog settled on his lap, he wrapped the blanket she'd brought around all three of them. She could not feel his body next to hers, nor Britta's.

They huddled there for what could have been anywhere from five minutes to a half hour, for all she knew. Her muscles pulsed with pain as the feeling slowly trickled back through her nerves.

"We're…alive," she finally managed.

Tanner chafed her shoulders, and she leaned her face against him. Now her cheek detected the stubble on his chin, his warm breath against her neck. It was a thrill to feel, to know the ice had not stripped away her senses permanently. She pressed close.

How grateful she felt at that moment that God had helped Tanner find her and brought them to shelter. There was no question she'd be dead if he and Britta hadn't intervened, but there was something else, another dimension to the comfort. She'd been going it alone, long before her days as a fugitive had begun. The pleasure and comfort of being near him was exquisite. She wanted to loop her arms around his neck and pour her emotions out. Instead she huddled there, tight to his side, and silently thanked the Lord for sending them, for Alice's courage in risking everything to help.

The half-buried trailer was the difference between life and death.

Tanner broke her reverie by withdrawing his arm. He stood with an effort that made him grimace, giving Britta the command to stay with Mara. Britta didn't need much convincing, burrowing tightly to Mara's side but she tracked her master intently. Mara stroked the dog's ears with her tingling hands and they shivered together. Was he headed for the door?

"Where are you going?" A rush of fear overtook her that he might leave, go for help in that monstrous storm. She wouldn't let him.

"Poking around, is all. See what we have to work with."

She exhaled a shaky breath.

She watched as he prowled the space and Mara could now see that the trailer appeared newer than she'd first suspected. A long rectangular space opened into two small sleeping areas at each end. In the middle was a tiny kitchenette with a gas stove and dining table with two narrow bench seats where she perched with Britta. There was a lone chair in the corner, the upholstery faded and worn. The Taj Mahal could not have been one bit lovelier, she thought. God had provided a palace, as far as she was concerned.

Tanner tapped the kitchen counter. "There's a gas stove so there must be a propane tank outside under all that snow. I'll dig it out in a minute."

Propane? Fuel meant heat and she could hardly make her mind believe it.

The window over the sink was covered by white blinds which Tanner made sure were closed before he opened two interior hallway doors. One revealed a cramped bathroom complete with a small shower and the other a closet.

"Yes." He pumped his fist and Britta wriggled her tail.

"What? Is it a radio or something?"

"No, it's even better. It's a power station." He knelt and looked closely at the switches. "This baby's got solar panels. I'll climb up and clear off the snow when I dig out the propane tank, but hopefully, the battery has enough stored energy to run the heater for a little while anyway."

Heater. She'd never heard a more glorious word. "What can I do?" she said through chattering teeth. "I will do literally anything to help you make that happen."

He smiled. There were still glimmers of ice in his hair. "Stay put and keep Britta warm." He handed her his phone. "Try to get a message to Asher. I don't think we're going to get a signal, but due diligence."

Since her frozen claws had turned back into usable fingers, she fiddled with the phone while he worked out how to turn on the power station.

He flipped switches and after a few clanks and buzzes, she heard the purr of a motor. He broke into a smile that lit his chapped face and wiped the shadows from under his eyes. "That, my fellow sojourner, is the sound of the heater kicking on."

"Praise the Lord."

"Believe me, I am."

She tried hard not to cry. Britta grazed her nose under Mara's chin. Not daring to speak, she watched Tanner free his collapsible shovel from his pack and go outside.

A bolt of terror shot through her. The storm, Eli...but she knew she could not give voice to her fear without dissolving. Instead she clamped her teeth together and listened. She heard him climb onto the roof and the soft thuds of snow falling off as he scraped it away. Britta followed his invisible progress with her nose as if they were magnetically linked. Not magnets, she thought fondly. Tanner and his faithful dog were attached at the heart level and always would be.

Warming her fingertips as best she could, she tried to dial Asher. The phone refused to cooperate, but her hopes stayed high. If the storm let up, they could replenish the trailer batteries, maybe hole up until they could get a call out. The relief of being out of the elements was dizzying, but she wouldn't completely relax until Tanner was back inside.

Gently easing Britta aside, Mara rose clumsily, feeling the tingling as the circulation was restored second by painful second. Pain was good. It meant frostbite hadn't killed off parts of her body. Another praise. She was certain they'd come uncomfortably close to losing fingers, toes or worse. Didn't take long for flesh to die in the conditions they'd just survived. If Britta hadn't been able to sniff out the trailer...

No sense dwelling on that thought. How could she help improve their situation? Shelter, check. Heat, possibly coming soon. On to the next two vital issues, food and water. Tanner's emergency backpack supplies would not hold out much longer. As her muscles gradually warmed, her stomach came to life with a growl.

Moving to the tiny kitchenette, she began checking the cupboards for food. Nothing in the first two, but the third yielded a bounty that made her squeal. Three cans of chicken noodle soup, unopened jars of peanut butter and strawberry jelly, a box of crackers and a six-pack of raisins. She waved the soup cans like maracas and twirled in an awkward dance. "Score," she cried out. Britta yipped in surprise and scampered over. Her happiness was compounded to see that the dog was moving without any sign of injury.

"Look what I found, Boo Bear?"

Britta rose up on her back legs to paw at Mara's thighs.

Another shelf held cans of tuna, pancake mix and an unopened tin of instant coffee. There was a small refrigerator, but it was the same temperature as the room, empty, as was the minuscule freezer compartment, save for a box of baking soda.

Tanner popped his head in, his knit cap furred with

snowflakes. "Propane tank's clear. God willing, we'll
have hot water and the stove will work. Be in soon."

It hurt to grin at him, but she did it anyway. When he
left again she realized she was thirsty, burningly so. No
doubt Britta and Tanner were too. There did not seem
to be any bottled water, and nothing came out of the
tap when she tried it, but if the stove was functional...

She turned the knob to the burner, delighted when it
clicked, sparked and glowed a soft orange. Flicking it off,
she found a pot. Tanner looked up in surprise from the
roof of the trailer when she forced her way outside. She
waved the pot and he gave her a thumbs-up. Though it
took her only a few seconds to pack the vessel with snow,
her joints screamed their displeasure. Tanner's shoulders were dusted with collected snow, and she wanted to
urge him to come down, but she knew he wouldn't until
he'd done what he set out to. His grit warmed her soul.

She remembered what he'd said about losing someone close to him and how he'd almost looked as though
he might hug her when she'd discussed her father.

Hugged? A simple act of compassion but the more
astonishing part was the disappointment she'd felt when
he didn't. She craved his touch, his comfort.

*Tanner is here because he was assigned to be. You're
working together to stay alive.* That was all. Didn't
matter if she'd come to realize her lone wolf attitudes
were holding her back, now wasn't the time to work on
changing that. Not now, not with Tanner. With renewed
purpose, she scrunched her way back.

Inside, she turned on the burner and held her hands
close while the snow in the pot melted. She wished Tanner would come back, but the stored energy in the bat-

teries would not last forever and the sun was all they could hope for to keep them in power. Still, he was risking frostbite, a fall, any number of dangers to restore the solar panels.

Those panels...

She pictured the glossy black panels she'd glimpsed while she was filling the pot. When the storm abated and the sun shone, those black surfaces would be soaking up the rays, but those very same rays would attract attention like a beacon for anyone who might be looking.

A shiny bullseye for Eli and Vinny to target? The snow in the pot dissolved with a hiss.

The meager warmth did not seem quite enough to dispel the freeze that took over her insides.

This bubble of safety was just that...a bubble. If they'd found the trailer, so could Eli.

Not could...would.

It was only a matter of when.

Tanner climbed off the roof and let himself back inside the trailer, locking the door and again checking to see that the blinds were all closed. The storm was showing signs of breaking up, and late afternoon shadows were creeping in, so he knew there was probably minimal risk of Eli spotting the solar panels. Hopefully they'd absorb a few rays before nightfall to complement the battery storage and keep the trailer powered.

He shook the snow from his clothes and accepted licks and wags from Britta as he checked her carefully from ears to tail. She appeared to have suffered no ill effects thanks to her insulated harness and the protection for her paws. He noticed Mara had provided her a bowl of boiled water and removed her booties. He pulled off her harness, providing a luxurious full body scratch that made her drop to the floor and flash her tummy. His knees complained as he knelt to oblige, but he did it anyway. Without question, they'd be dead if it weren't for this courageous, faithful dog. An angel in a fur coat, he was convinced. He showered her with kisses.

"You're my good Boo Bear," he crooned.

Mara was stirring two pots on the stove as he went to stand next to the heating vent, desperate to absorb some of the warmth. She offered him a cup of luke-warm water which he glugged down without delay. His nostrils quivered, picking up an enticing aroma from the second pot.

"That smells incredible."

She laughed and poured the contents into two large mugs. "I figure this way we can feel the warmth better while we eat." The trailer was still extremely cold, and he was delighted with her plan. She held up a red plastic bowl. "I poured some kibble in from your backpack for Britta. Is it okay if I add a teaspoon of soup?"

Britta, hearing her name and spying the bowl, began to squirm all over with anticipation and that had to be a smile on those fleshy boxer lips. He laughed. "How could I say no after what she did for us today? Dog deserves a prime rib dinner when we get back and she's going to get it."

Mara set the bowl on the floor and refilled Britta's water bowl with more boiled snowmelt. Britta sat obediently, waiting for Tanner to give her permission.

"Chow time." The dog raced to the bowls and began

a noisy meal. It did his heart good to see her enthusiasm. He felt the same about his mug of soup. If he had a tail, he'd be wagging it as he slid onto the bench seat at the table. "Any progress with the phone?"

She shook her head and joined him. "No, sorry to say."

He held his face over the soup and cupped the mug with one hand. She surprised him by taking his other, kneading his cold fingers.

Her eyes were so brilliant, like gemstones. Her fingers teased warmth into his. Her touch filtered through him, sunshine on snow. How could simple human contact fill up his heart in such a way?

She said a simple grace, full of thanksgiving, her voice breaking until she was unable to continue.

"Thank You, Lord and amen," he finished for her.

He was filled with a similar gratitude and something else he couldn't describe, some strange emotion that anchored him there in that feeling of…what? Comfort? Intimacy? Too nebulous to label. He gulped soup to cover his confusion. The salty broth soothed his raw throat and made his taste buds sing. "Absolutely the finest meal ever to cross my palate."

Mara drank and rolled her eyes. "Agreed. I am totally writing the soup company to tell them they are the bee's knees."

He laughed. "I'll sign it too, and Britta will give her paw print endorsement."

Mara gave him a rundown of the supplies. He grinned. Better than he could have hoped for.

She jotted a note on a crumpled piece of paper. "I'm keeping a list so we know how much to reimburse Alice."

Practical. Ethical. He liked that. How many other women would have thought of that in such a situation? "Still no phone success?"

"Sorry, no. But I'll keep trying."

Now that they were out of the elements, he could see her clearly. There was a scratch on her cheek, and her dark hair glimmered with moisture. Everything about her was so vivid, so…alive. Why did he want to study her, every flicker of expression and nuance of feeling? Facing death together had probably brought more vibrancy to the situation, he told himself. Natural.

She tapped her pencil on the table. "And if we bring in more snow, it will melt by morning so we won't have to use the stove in case the propane is low. Will the batteries keep the trailer going for a while?"

"We'll have to hope so." He checked his watch. "Why does it feel like midnight? It's only four o'clock."

"Because this has been an absolutely endless day."

"You got that right. Seems like a lifetime since Eli found my car. Soon as the storm breaks I'm going to hike for a while and see if I can get a signal on my phone and at least send a text out."

She sighed and sipped the remains of her soup. Sorrow replaced the optimism. She chewed her lip.

"What is it?" he found himself asking, surprised how much he wanted to decipher her turn of mood. Decipher and ease the pain away. He shifted uneasily.

"I'm sorry I got you and Britta into this mess, Tanner. Sincerely, sorry. If I'd made different choices…"

He shrugged. "You know how many times I've said that, Mara?"

"It's been my constant thought since I bolted. I can't

seem to remember how I used to feel before I ran from the murder scene. All of it is one big painful blur. I think I was cocky, mostly. Figured I could do things alone, didn't really need anyone nor made much of an attempt to get to know the people around me."

"You were reserved, is all. Nothing wrong with that."

"Except that when it came down to it, I didn't give people a reason to trust me. They didn't really know who I was because I didn't let them."

She could have been describing his life. He chose his words carefully. "There is one thing I wondered about that we haven't discussed. The chief called your cell right after the murders." He waited for her reply.

Her gaze roved his face. "And you wonder why I didn't answer?"

"I mean if you could trust anybody, it'd be him, right?" Chief Donovan Fanelli was the unit's rock, the man that was a spokesperson for integrity.

A few moments ticked by and she found her voice. "I could say it was panic. I'd just seen my former boyfriend lying dead next to Stacey Stark. When Danica and Colt arrived at the scene, I thought about calling out to them, then I considered it from a crime tech's viewpoint. I was on scene. Eli dropped my bracelet nearby. I'd had a public disagreement with Jonas right after we broke up a month ago. I knew nothing would support my innocence. Plus there was Eli's threat to my dad. But I've been thinking about why I didn't trust the chief or the team and really at the core, I think it came down to the fact that I didn't give anyone an opportunity to know me, not really." She traced a circle on the table with her fingertip. "I didn't think they'd really want to, actually."

He goggled. Not at all what he'd expected her to say. "That's why you didn't answer the chief?"

"I know it sounds nutty, but like I said I've had a lot of time to ponder this. I didn't think Chief Fanelli would actually *want* to help me, nor would most of the rest of the team." She heaved out a breath. "I have some… trust issues, I guess."

He yearned to hear more, but it would be her choice to share or not. He let another swallow of hot soup trace a warm path to his stomach, willing her to keep sharing. *Tell me what makes you tick, Mara.* The need for answers burned him like a live coal.

"My father cheated on Asher's mother when Asher was ten. They divorced and Dad started a new relationship with my mother and they had me. That whole messy episode was a complete bombshell which I didn't know about until I was almost sixteen and my mother had been dead for years. Dad became a Christian right after my mother died, but still it took him a long time to finally tell me the truth. Dad carried a lot of deep shame about that, and he sort of shut down." She pulled out the keychain photo and showed him, a smiling Mara next to her father wearing a fuzzy yellow sweater.

"How did you react, hearing that your father had a whole other family? That he cheated?" He couldn't imagine. His own parents were the most honorable people he knew.

"For a while, I really struggled, but it explained a lot of things. We were kind of a solitary family, except for some school activities. I was raised to be self-sufficient and private and that's kind of my personality too, but hearing that made me more so. I've always been wary of relationships. I assume people don't want to get to know me. It gives me an excuse to keep them at arm's length."

Who on earth wouldn't want to know Mara? *You didn't.* The thought pained him. He'd wanted to and if he hadn't gone through losing Allie maybe…

She stowed the photo. "I did that with the people on the team, the chief, and…" She tapped a finger on her mug. "And you. I definitely told myself that you didn't want to know me very deeply." She shrugged. "It probably explains why Jonas and I didn't make it too. I've come to figure out that's a 'me' issue more than anything."

Her honesty elicited a response he hadn't planned. "No, it wasn't all you. I stopped opening myself up to people after my fiancée died."

Now it was her turn to look surprised, the expression captured by the weak light further cut by the closed blinds.

"I didn't know about your fiancée. I'm sorry."

He nodded a thanks, wishing he could put the words back inside where they belonged. Sharing was messy and painful, like picking a wound that hadn't fully scabbed over. "Happened four years ago so… It was a long, protracted hideously painful experience. I decided I didn't ever want to feel that way again." Why was he telling her this? He was desperate to change the subject, steer them back on safe ground. "But I guess I understand why you didn't want to answer the chief's call. You reached out to Asher and Willow though, I know. Then no more contact?"

"Only that one additional call I made from a gas station phone when I gave Asher the clue about where to find me. I should have tried to make contact earlier, but I couldn't risk it. Eli was everybody's friend, and I didn't want to cause any trouble for my brother or Willow. They'd have to disclose any conversations we had since I was the person of interest in the murders."

If Asher had been more open…if she'd been able to trust him…

"I never would have imagined how it would turn out." There was a slight tone of uncertainty in her voice. She still doubted her decisions, doubted herself.

"You don't have to justify your actions to me. I get it. Given the choice, I'd always pick going it alone too."

She took another sip, draining her soup. "Before, I would have said we had that in common, but I've changed my mind about it. I think God's been teaching me through this debacle that alone isn't always best."

Might not be best, he thought, but it had to be better than the agony he'd experienced. Alone was painful. Together could be excruciating. "Hard to know what's best." It was clear by the way she leaned back a fraction that he'd redrawn the distance between them. A vicious gust of wind rattled the trailer. "How about we get settled in for the night?"

She found a couple of blankets and shared one with him. He and Britta took the bed on one end of the trailer and her the other. The view out his window from behind the blinds was limited, but he scoped it out nonetheless, feeling Mara looking at him.

"I'll keep watch. Don't worry."

"You stayed up last night when we were in the car. You need to sleep."

"I'm…"

She interrupted. "You watch until midnight. I'll wake up and take my shift from then until the morning."

He shook his head.

"I know we both like to go it alone, Tanner, but this requires teamwork if we're going to make it."

"I'm really not that tired."

"And you're not a good liar either."

Why was she pushing so hard? Irritation strummed his nerves. "Mara…"

"Do you trust me?"

The question seemed to hang in the soup-scented air. Trust her? It wasn't a matter of knowing she would stay awake for the watch. He knew her question went deeper. Was he willing to open himself up enough to put his heart in her hands? He thought he'd explained that a moment before. No, he wasn't, but he didn't want to hurt her by flat out saying so. He realized he'd waited too long to reply, which was answer enough.

She stepped back, wrapping her arms around herself, smaller somehow than she'd been a moment before.

"There's a timer in the kitchen. I'll set an alarm for midnight to relieve you." She turned around and trudged to her side of the trailer.

Spirit sinking, he made his way to his with Britta following along.

If I could trust anyone, it'd be you, Mara.

The words remained unspoken as he settled into sleep.

SIX

Mara slept, waking with a thundering heart until she reacclimated herself to the present. They were in a trailer. She was safe, warm and sleeping on an honest-to-goodness mattress. How strange. Stranger yet, Tanner Ford and Britta were occupying the trailer with her. After so long on her own, she found herself filled with a strange longing. She yearned to keep talking, to open herself up to another person, to Tanner. Sharing was a novel and exhilarating experience. Sharing with Tanner was a deeper level of satisfaction, as if they were uniquely suited for each other. *Watch your step, Mara.*

She shouldn't submerge herself too deeply with Tanner. That point was hammered home in the question she'd asked him.

Do you trust me?

His non-answer was evidence. No, he didn't. And why should he anyway? He'd flat out told her he'd always prefer going it alone. Seven months before she would have agreed with him. When the clock meandered its way to midnight, she wrapped herself in a blanket and padded to the kitchen where Tanner sat in the only chair, Britta curled at his feet.

The dog perked up at her approach, though the room was dark. They'd not wanted to advertise their presence or drain the battery by activating the light. Tanner acknowledged her with a nod.

She offered a mock salute. "Reporting for duty, Officer Tanner."

He sighed. "All right. I'd rather you got to sleep all night but to be honest I've had to resort to doing push-ups to keep myself awake. Let me know if you hear or see anything."

"I will."

He looked as though he wanted to say more, but instead he turned and left with Britta. She heard the mattress creak as he climbed up. The man had to be exhausted, mentally and physically. And he'd been trying to track her location along with the rest of the team in the time she'd been on the run. How much she'd missed.

And how much she'd changed.

She situated herself at the kitchen table where she could peek through the blinds, unwilling to risk disturbing Tanner by fixing a cup of instant coffee. The wind was still blowing hard, but not as violently, which meant the storm was abating, this wave of it at least. It would be easier to get around.

Easier for them…and for Eli and Vinny.

The thought gave her extra vigilance as she kept watch. The hours passed slowly, but she did not mind. Tanner was sleeping and she was content that she'd given him the opportunity, that he'd grudgingly entrusted her with watch duty.

Not really a matter of trust—he'd had no choice. If they were going to survive until help arrived, he and

Britta needed to recharge. Minutes ticked into hours, and she did silent laps around the kitchen when her muscles cramped. When the time on her watch crept close to dawn, she couldn't sit anymore. As quietly as she could, she poured some of the boiled water into a smaller pot and turned on the burner, adding a couple of hefty tablespoons of instant coffee which made her senses tingle. Was there a finer aroma on earth than the smell of coffee on a frigid winter morning? She sipped, washed so deeply in a memory that she didn't hear Tanner's approach until he cleared his throat. She screamed, sloshing some coffee on her shirt.

"Sorry." He held up his palms. "I didn't mean to scare you. I thought I was dreaming the coffee smell."

She apologized for waking him and fixed him a cup, enjoying the expression of bliss on his face when he inhaled the steam from the mug. Britta greeted Mara and got an ear rub in return.

"Time to get up anyway." He drank. "You were pretty deep in thought there."

"Actually I was remembering Jonas."

"Oh. That must have been, uh, painful, to find him there...with..." Tanner's cheeks went rosy and he swigged a big swallow of coffee that likely burned his mouth.

"With Stacey? Yes, for several reasons, but probably not the ones you think. It was terrible seeing them murdered. I'll never wash it from my mind." She swallowed hard. "I've been at many crime scenes of course, but seeing the man you'd dated..."

"Yeah." A wisp of steam floated up from his coffee mug. "There were some theories floated around by the unit at first that it was a murder motivated by, er, jealousy."

She shook her head. "I might have thought that too if I was the one investigating. But there was no jealousy on my part. Jonas and I broke up the month before he was murdered. I didn't take it well at first. He'd said we just didn't seem to be a pair, and I felt so betrayed, unworthy, even though he was as gentle as he could be."

"There were those reports that you'd had a public argument."

Was Tanner's curiosity professional? Or something else? "True, we did, but not because I was still in love with him." She pulled in a deep breath and exhaled. Before she would have avoided the question. No more. "I was furious because I found out he started seeing Stacey immediately after he broke up with me. I jumped to this enormous conclusion that he'd been cheating on me, maybe because of what happened with my dad and Asher's mother. It was difficult to trust Jonas with my past, and then to imagine he'd not had the nerve to be honest with me." She flashed back on the argument at the coffee shop, his inability to meet her eye when she'd confronted him.

"I deserved to know, Jonas."

"There was nothing to know. I didn't see anyone else while we were dating and that's the truth."

"You could have told me you met someone."

"I didn't, Mara. Not until after." He'd taken her hand and she'd felt her anger give way to deep pain as she realized he was telling the truth. He hadn't cheated on her, he'd merely stopped loving her. That one angry conversation with Jonas made her understand her half brother a little bit better, how betrayal had rippled through their

family and shaded their own ability to trust and be trusted. "It was a mortifying scene and Jonas didn't deserve it. Didn't deserve anything bad and it horrifies me to think that the man who murdered them both has been walking around free all this time, threatening my father, Asher, me." Why was her throat thick with unexpressed tears all of a sudden? It was as if their respite from danger had cut loose all the thoughts that had swirled inside like a tempest. So much pain, injustice.

Tanner put his coffee down and removed her mug from her shaking fingers before he enveloped her in an embrace. The tears did flow then, pouring out and onto his chest as he squeezed her. His gesture surprised and delighted her, allowed the grief to release like steam from a boiling kettle. She wanted to stay there and listen to the quiet, steady thud of his heart.

"I'm sorry for what you've been through," he whispered, his lips grazing her ear. "We can't erase that stuff, but you're going to get home safe, back to the team, and your brother and Willow."

She leaned closer, suddenly desperate for his comfort as the painful past washed over her afresh. She'd been sobbing that day after her confrontation with Jonas, angry at herself for accusing him. She'd called Willow who'd been working and unable to return her call. She'd thought that was a new low point for her life, but she'd had no idea that worse was yet to come, much worse.

He held her until she was able to gather herself. "I'm sorry. Didn't mean to cry all over your shirt." She accepted a concerned poke from Britta. "I wanted so badly to talk through it with Willow, but I never got the chance." She cocked her head. "How is she?"

He grinned. "I forgot you didn't know."

"Know what?"

"Willow and Theo are expecting."

"Really?" Mara squeaked. "They reconciled?" She clapped a hand over her mouth. "Forget I said that." It was such a painful situation for the two, and her friend had revealed her marital troubles under strictest confidence. "I missed so much in seven months. I can't wait to see her. Oh, my gosh, a baby."

"Baby's due in December so you'll be able to get up to speed when we get home."

Home. For a split second she wondered what it would be like to return to her previous life. Would she really be welcomed back to the team? By her friend? And her brother? It wasn't just Willow's life that had gone on in the months she'd been away. Everyone's had, and she'd be stepping back into that world. She realized he'd put a hand on her shoulder.

"It's a lot to think about, but it will all work out when you get back into your normal rhythms."

She'd craved those normal rhythms, but she knew she wouldn't be able to resume with the barriers in place she'd had before. "I—I just hope Asher and I can be real siblings, for a change. We've missed out on so much already."

He squeezed her forearm. "I know that's what he wants too." The stubble on Tanner's chin lent him an air of ruggedness, accentuated by the intense brown of his eyes.

She smiled, suddenly awkward at being so close to this handsome man who was both a friend and a stranger and tried to lighten the mood. "How about you? Any exciting developments in your life during my time as a desperate fugitive? Fill me in. Any relationships brewing?"

She regretted the words as soon as they came out of her mouth. Tanner was private; he'd said as much. And unwilling to enter into romances after his fiancée died. He'd made that clear too. And here she was asking about his love life.

He smiled but she saw the shutters drop across his face. "Nah. Same old quiet life for me."

The way he stepped back from her underscored the words. Detached from relationships and detached from her. *So no more nosy questions, Mara.* She nodded and concentrated on draining her mug to the dregs.

He put down his coffee. "I'm going to climb to the peak behind us before sunrise. See if I can get a signal."

"I'll come."

"No. You stay here. No need for us both to get cold. Britta and I will handle it."

Alone. Like he wanted.

"All right." She wasn't quite sure why it stung as she watched him head to the door without her. "Wait."

He turned and she pulled up the bench seat, exposing a storage space underneath, and extracted two pairs of snowshoes. His utter delight thrilled her.

"How'd you find these?"

She grinned. "You do push-ups to stay awake, I snoop through trailers. I even found the owner's manual to read with my morning coffee and a couple other treasures."

He took a pair and tucked them under his arm. "This is really going to help. Thank you."

She'd helped. That would have to be enough.

* * *

An hour and a half later, Tanner returned from his arduous climb, anxious to rejoin Mara and get his dog out of the bitter cold. The back of his neck prickled. There had been no outward signs of danger, but he felt it, nonetheless, a threat swirling around them like the storm. After he schooled his expression into something neutral, he stomped the accumulation off his snowshoes and removed them. He let himself inside and took off Britta's booties. She shook herself clear of the bits of snow, sprinkling him and Mara.

Her green eyes searched his. "Did you find a place where you could get a signal?"

He chafed life back into his fingers. "No, unfortunately. I thought I had a few bars at one point, and I wrote a text to Asher, but it didn't send."

Her mouth crimped in disappointment. "I suppose it would have been too much to hope for if you found that perfect sweet spot, called the team and they were helicoptering in at this very moment."

"Yeah. That'd be too good to be true."

They stood in the kitchen listening to the snow sloughing in piles off the roof. She waited for him to continue. He appreciated that Mara was as thoughtful and deliberate as he was. He blew on his fingertips. "We need to talk about options."

"That sounds ominous."

"Just a fallback position if the trailer is compromised. I learned in Alaska that a couple of minutes of preplanning can sometimes save your life."

She nodded. "My dad says act in haste, repent in leisure. Unfortunately, I haven't always had the luxury of planning time with Eli on my tail, but I try to remember Dad's lesson." She poured two mugs of hot coffee and they sat at the table. "Where do you get your cautious streak from?"

"Learning from my rookie mistakes, mostly. My parents run a floatplane business in Homer. In spite of everything they harped on about safety, I decided one time at the ripe old age of seventeen I was a good enough pilot to fly to a glacier to see the northern lights. Got the plane stuck in a crevice and fractured my ankle all in one fell swoop. Cell phone had no connection and I didn't have a backup radio or satellite phone. Would have died there if my dad hadn't gotten me out. My folks had the good grace not to ever tease me about it since they knew how shaken up I was, but my younger sister razzed me forever, which I deserved. Siblings keep egos in check, that's for sure."

"Funny, but I always wished I had a sibling to joke around with." Her smile faded. Impulsively, he took her hand and squeezed her fingers, so warm against his cold skin.

"Plenty of sibling teasing ahead in your future, don't worry. Asher will make up for lost time when we get back. Probably thinking up pranks and annoying nicknames even as we speak."

She returned the squeeze, cradling his hand between her palms and rubbing to help the circulation. "You're like ice."

The touch was overwhelming, exciting and somehow natural at the same time. Confusion and comfort danced inside him. He wanted to pull her into an embrace, but his arms had been empty since Allie died and he wanted it to stay that way. Didn't he? He swallowed and tried to corral the feelings until she let go. Britta scuttled over and he hoisted her up onto the seat next to him. She laid her head on his lap and he stroked the satin of her ears. She always reset him.

Mara tucked a section of hair behind her ear and sat straighter. Business time. "Okay. You mentioned options. Do you have some in mind?"

"I thought of a bunch of them, but none sound fantastic."

"What are the choices as you see them?"

"Stay here, keep hiking around to find a spot where I can get a call out to Asher and the team. The advantages are obvious. We have food for a couple of days, warmth, hot water, shelter. All huge plusses. There's another storm front coming and we'd be able to ride that out in relative safety and comfort if we hunker down here."

She nodded. "The word *comfort* puts a skip in my step but the downside is we're sitting ducks if Eli finds us and the clock is ticking until he spots the solar panels."

"Exactly, so on to option two. According to my initial research before I arrived, there's a bed-and-breakfast about twenty miles from here. One of those hike-in places, geared for outdoorsy types. Even if it's closed up due to the blizzard, they'd have to have a generator and a communication system. We could pack supplies, head there, and hope for decent weather."

She nodded. "I think I stayed there once, but that was nearly twenty years ago. Forgot all about it. I remember it was rustic and definitely remote."

"It's going to be a haul and it'd take two, maybe three

days to reach it, depending on the storm and our speed. Hard going, even with snowshoes and we'd be vulnerable to injury and hypothermia."

She shot him a mischievous smile. "Actually, I might be able to sweeten that option."

"How's that?"

"Two reasons. First, I know of an old campground a little more than halfway between here and the B and B," she said. "Dad and I went there a couple of times when we couldn't get into the other campgrounds. Probably not much left of it. When I was running from Olympia, I stopped at a church and I heard someone reminiscing with a friend about it and he said a handful of the tent cabins are still standing. We could stop there as a midpoint. Rest if the storm worsens. Britta would be able to alert if Eli gets close."

"Good to know. And the second reason?"

She picked up a paper from the counter and handed it to him with a triumphant grin. "As I told you, I found the manual in the drawer that goes with the trailer and I read all fifteen pages of it. Turns out, this rig has a covered compartment in the bottom, a kind of built-in garage just big enough for a…" She trailed off dramatically.

His eyes rounded. "Are you kidding me? A vehicle?"

"A snowmobile."

He sprang up, ready to head for the door, but she stopped him. "I already checked while you were out. It's there. Safe and sound. There's about a half tank of gas and no extra that I can find, so I'm thinking we could maybe even reach the B and B in one day if there are no hiccups. Running the engine will be noisy but the winds might help cover the sound. We'll have to return it and reimburse Alice for the gasoline and wear and tear, but desperate times, right?"

The grin spread across his face now. "Right. That's an incredible find. I wouldn't have thought to scan the trailer specs. You're a genius."

Her cheeks turned an enticing shade of pink. "We're partners, right? I'm not going to sit around idle while you risk your safety and Britta's out there. We'll have to hope the engine noise doesn't carry. Did you see any signs of Eli?"

"No."

Her arched eyebrow indicated she'd detected something in his tone. Mara was insightful, and she didn't miss the tiniest detail. It made her a great crime scene investigator. Admiration ballooned inside him. Again, he shoved it down. Britta slid off his lap and sidled over, blowing out her fleshy lips as Mara stroked her head.

"You're the best dog in the world, Britta. Have I told you that today?"

Britta licked her wrist. The dog was friendly, but she didn't always take to people the way she was attaching to Mara. Britta trusted that Mara would not hurt her.

What would that be like, to love and trust wholeheartedly without fear of the pain that came with it? He wished he could do the same, but dogs knew nothing of the agony that lingered when someone was ripped out of a person's life. They lived in the moment, unworried, unanchored in the past or future.

It occurred to Tanner in that moment, that his own existence was anchored firmly in the past. The grief that had washed over him in a relentless tide had not drowned him because he'd held himself firmly in place until it passed him by.

But happiness had rushed on past too.

He realized while his thoughts were flying off into la-la land, Mara was silently waiting for him to continue.

"As I said, I didn't have any concrete indications that we are in immediate danger here."

"That's a very cautiously worded statement, Officer."

Allie always had that same way of seeing below the surface. Why was he perpetually thinking of Allie? He cleared his throat. "I can't in good conscience lead us into a possible freezing-to-death scenario when we're safe here."

"But…?"

"But Eli is smart, and he's not going to leave until he's finished things." *Finished them all.*

"I agree. It's a matter of time…how much do we have before he finds us?"

"Impossible to know, but he and Vinny have shelter, access to fuel, food, et cetera, or they couldn't have pursued us this far. Eli mentioned a camper, so it's gotta be somewhere central and if it's still functional, they've got a massive advantage. Plus they're going to know as soon as we get communication in place, the team will deploy to find us. If he's anywhere close, the moment we start up that snowmobile, he'll be on us like a dog on a biscuit."

"Stay or go?" Mara's mouth pursed into a bow. "The same question I've been mulling over for seven months. Doesn't get easier."

Again he marveled. She'd been living a brutal day-to-day, maybe hour-to-hour existence. What kind of strength had it taken for her to survive it?

They fell into silence. He realized the joint problem solving was invigorating him. It felt completely natural. Puzzling. Some shared survival phenomenon?

Together.

The word made him squirm. He'd vowed there'd be no together with anyone ever again. *Been there, done that, paid the price.* This was merely a togetherness born of extreme circumstances.

"I've been scouting too, today," she said. "Behind the trailer through the woods there's a gradual slope that becomes pretty steep. No way for Eli and Vinny to operate snowmobiles on such a terrain. If they cut us off from the front and we can't get to our snowmobile, we could snowshoe out that way. Having a back door escape route might make it possible for us to wait here a few hours more. How are you at snowmobiling at night?"

"It's not optimal, but I had a fair amount of practice in Alaska and I only broke a bone once."

"Ha-ha. Very funny."

"If we decide to go, I think we should wait until dark. Storm isn't leaving anytime soon so we'll have some cover."

"I'll pack our supplies up so we can be ready to escape out the back way at the first sign of trouble and keep an eye out in case Eli and Vinny try to hike in and surprise us." The snow drove past the window, swirling shadows of light and dark. Mara sighed. "I hope it's not my mind rationalizing because my body is so happy to be warm for a few more hours."

"Nothing wrong with being warm. As a matter of

fact, I was going to suggest you nab a hot shower. Might be the last opportunity for a while." He almost gulped at Mara's smile. He recalled Allie's bliss when the nurses would allow her to use the hospital shower.

"*The restorative powers of hot water, Tanny*," she'd crowed.

"I've had precisely one hot shower since I went on the run, at a church that provided help like that. It was the only time I knew Eli wouldn't catch me by surprise since there were people standing guard."

He patted Britta. "Consider yourself guarded. Your brother would insist on nothing less than a canine detail, just like he did for…" *Shut your mouth, Tanner.* It was too late.

Mara pounced on his slip of the tongue. "Who?"

He became busy patting his pockets for his gloves. "Oh, uh, nothing."

"Not nothing. What are you not telling me?"

"Uh, well, really, I…" He got up, as if in search of coffee.

She followed suit, folding her arms. "Listen, buster. I'm not a crime scene tech for nothing. I know a clue when I see one. Spill it."

He sighed. "I figured maybe your brother would want to tell you in person."

She crossed her arms. "That's like waving a pot roast in front of a bear. You have to tell me now or it's going to get ugly up in here."

He sighed. Trapped by his own big mouth. "Asher and Peyton are engaged."

Mara's jaw dropped. "Peyton Burns? The dog trainer for our unit? She and Asher?"

"Yep. They got pretty close working on a case where they impersonated a married couple and what do you know? Their cover became their reality."

Mara's hands flew to her mouth, and she actually hopped up and down. Britta leaped up too, paws scrabbling the air to join in the merriment. "Asher and Peyton… it's like a TV movie."

He laughed and so did she. They chuckled together until Mara wiped her eyes. "The truth is stranger than fiction, right? I would say I can't believe it, but knowing their personalities, they're pretty compatible. I am so excited. When's the wedding?"

"Asher said they won't set a firm date until you get home."

She inhaled sharply. "He's…waiting for me?"

"He and Peyton both agreed."

Tears glazed her eyes and her mouth trembled. "For a long time," she choked out, "I prayed that Asher would love me."

"Prayer answered," Tanner said, with a sigh. The old wound tugged at his insides.

Mara cocked her head. "Memories?"

Normally he'd shrug off the comment, insert a joke or change the subject. Something about her made him switch gears and answer as honestly as he could. "I was thinking that at the end of Allie's life when the doctors had tried everything, I stopped praying for her healing and began asking God to give me the suffering and take it away from her." He blinked. "My prayer was answered. Her pain went away but mine never did, until lately." Until lately? Why had he added those two words? He stood frozen, searching for a way to explain it to her, to himself.

She cocked her head, the same question written in her expression.

He wished he could flee outside and jump in the nearest snowbank. "I meant that I've been thinking about what you said, that shutting everyone out of my life probably isn't the best for my soul."

She beamed. "Took me a while to get to that conclusion."

"Guess I'm slower to get there than you." He tapped his forehead. "Not as sharp."

"It's harder for introverts like us."

Us. Britta trotted over, flopped on her tummy and bicycled her legs for a scratch. The conversation gushed out of him. "This dog is smarter than I am, for sure. She's never really let me be alone from the day I got her." Another surge of pain tore at his insides. "Allie loved dogs too. We were going to buy a property off the grid in Alaska after we got married. Raise lots of dogs and garden in the summer. Had it all written up. I'd work for the Alaska PD and she'd do her computer programming online. We had it detailed right down to what we'd stock in the pantry. Lots of raviolis. Allie loved the kind that came in the can."

"That sounds like a beautiful plan."

Beautiful, and wasted. "A daydream, is all." He checked his phone to give himself something to do besides look at her pity-filled expression. *Why share? It just makes her feel sorry for you.* This wasn't the time, nor place. "Anyway, I'd better get out there and check on things."

"You seem to read the weather better than I can. How much of a break from the storm do you think we'll get?"

"I'd say there will be some slacking off by tonight." Catch-22. The darkness would bring better weather.

But it would also be when the hunters would come out. Their cushion of safety wouldn't last. His gut told him danger was approaching. *Don't get comfortable, Tanner.*

Mara's laughter was rich and warm as she knelt, and Britta licked her face. The sound rolled through him like a soft mountain rain. It was followed by a storm of unease.

Definitely, not too comfortable.

SEVEN

Mara chewed on her conversation with Tanner as she let stinging water inject warmth into her body. If it was possible to store up heat and comfort, she intended to try her best to do both. With no hair dryer to be found, she didn't risk shampooing her thick hair. It would not do to be on the run in freezing temps with wet hair. Soon they would be battling the elements again, but hopefully it would be the final leg of the sprint for survival. The danger hadn't lessened one iota, but her spirit was more buoyant than it had been since April.

The shower washed another thought to the top. It wasn't simply the trailer and the hot water and food that soothed her soul. It was Tanner. Why, she wondered? Regret, perhaps, that she'd never allowed herself to relax her defenses around him. Never tried to push through their easygoing, surface level banter. She hadn't been willing to risk getting to know him or anybody, but Eli's pursuit had peeled away all her pretensions and exposed a deep need to be authentic. Tanner with his quiet intelligence and deep reservoir of feelings attracted her like a warm ray of sunlight on a winter day. The new Mara realized she'd lost too many opportunities already.

She jerked off the taps. *Don't go getting yourself confused. He's here to get you home. He's told you he won't love someone else after Allie, so shut down that line of thinking pronto, missy.*

Dried, dressed, blissfully warm and clean, she double-checked the backpack and supplies she'd stowed and wrote a note with the PKN9's contact information so Alice could reach out for reimbursement, affixing it with a magnet to the tiny fridge. On the counter, the opened box of pancake mix caught her attention. They'd need every calorie they could pack down to complete their arduous journey. There would be no way to cook after they left the trailer, but premade pancakes could be wrapped in foil and would be lightweight enough to carry along. A smart idea, she figured. Who knew when they'd have a chance to restock their food supplies? The biggest problem was that she couldn't wrap up the delicious warmth of the trailer and take it along, but she had some ideas about that too.

After lighting the gas stove, she put a pan on to heat and stirred together the mix and water. When the cast iron sizzled, she grabbed a potholder to steady it while she poured in big spoonfuls of batter. After the pancakes had turned golden brown, she wrapped them in foil and stowed the warm bundle in her backpack. One more batch to go.

She was about to ladle in more batter when she heard Britta bark, loud and intense. The trailer floor vibrated. Someone was approaching fast. The door slammed open. Tanner and Britta charged in.

"Get down," he shouted, shutting the door and bolting it.

Mara dropped the potholder and fell to her knees.

Bullets sprayed through the trailer windows, chips of glass biting into her scalp. Eli and Vinny. She'd not heard snowmobiles. They must have come on foot.

You let your guard down. When will you learn?

Tanner yanked his weapon free. He popped up and fired through the fractured glass as another hail of bullets slammed in, gouging holes in the cupboards and tattering the curtains. The blast pierced her eardrums.

Tanner gestured to Britta and she belly crawled over to Mara. "Take Britta and go out the back. Get away from here."

"Not without you."

His brow furrowed. "We're not going down this road again. I'll buy you some time to get away. You have to go."

"Eli knows my general location now, Tanner. I won't survive by myself. I need you and Britta. Nothing has changed." And she desperately did not want Tanner to wage a losing war against Eli. He would die at the hands of a man who had already ended two lives and would harm her father to get what he wanted. No scruples, no mercy. She couldn't allow that. A bullet sailed into the kitchen, clanging against the cast iron pan and letting a spark loose before it ricocheted and bored into the ceiling. An acrid smell of smoke burned her nostrils.

He turned a tortured look at her, mouth twisted. "Mara, go…"

She tipped her chin up, touching Britta for encouragement. "Give me a count, then we all make a break for it." She knew he would acquiesce. He had to. Part of her felt bad about forcing his hand, but not bad enough to change her mind. Another shot sizzled through the trailer and blew apart a cupboard door, spewing wood fragments down around them. She barely contained her scream.

While Tanner darted a look out the window, she grabbed the backpack and both sets of snowshoes. The potholder had touched the burner and ignited sending up a yellow flame. Smoke filled the trailer. There was no time to worry about that now.

Tanner returned fire again. He crawled across the floor, hooked the chair and dragged it to the front door, jamming it under the handle. "This will only buy us minutes. They'll check the back."

She thrust the snowshoes at him. "Then we'd better make the most of the minutes." She shoved open the rear door, sat on the steps and strapped on the snowshoes. Within seconds she hopped off, Tanner took one more shot and did the same. Snow was falling steadily, the wind shrieking in the pines. Tanner faced Britta and pointed to the dense forest.

"Away."

Britta pranced off, booties whisking through the snow. The dog knew Eli's scent and she also knew they had gained as much distance from it as possible.

Tanner urged Mara ahead of him, their floundering first steps evening out as they found a rhythm with their snowshoes. Another rattle of bullets plowed into the trailer behind them, sending a piece of the solar panel whirling through the air. Her muscles in her back and shoulders tightened. The next bullets might find them.

Heads down, they soldiered on in Britta's wake.

The subsequent shots were swallowed up by a whooshing sound. They jerked as an explosion split the sky, vibrating the snow under their feet. An orange plume of flame erupted from the top of the trailer.

"What happened?" she whispered.

"A bullet must have caught the gas line and the burning potholder added the heat."

Her heart squeezed as the trailer that had saved their lives began to burn. Alice had risked so much to get them here. Mara hoped the falling snow would snuff out the flames before it was a total loss. Had Eli and Vinny been near the explosion? Were they dead? Wounded?

Tanner took her hand. "Might help us. Delay their pursuit if the explosion didn't catch them. Let's go."

As she struggled along, he took the heavy pack from her shoulders, adding it to the one he already carried.

She didn't argue. It was all she could do to maintain their rapid pace through the trees. Her thoughts churned in frantic circles. If Vinny and Eli hadn't been injured, perhaps the explosion would make them worry about drawing attention, if there was anyone around in such tumultuous weather. There was no way they could stop to check on their pursuers. She clomped along, focused on putting one clumsy foot in front of the other, avoiding rocks and fallen branches swaddled in white. Her breath came in frozen puffs and the driving flakes cut at her cheeks. Tanner grabbed her arm when she foundered and, strangely, tugged her off their chosen path toward two towering crags.

"Wrong way," she called over the wind.

Tanner ignored her comment and moved with purpose. Britta hesitated, ears cocked, waiting for Mara. Worried that Tanner was confused, she followed. Their unexpected segue was veering them nearer to the trailer, not farther away.

When they drew closer to a massive snow-covered ridge, he paused to pull off his snowshoes before propelling her toward a narrow, rocky gap. In a daze, she removed her snowshoes. What was he thinking? Leading them back toward Eli? Finding a hiding place amidst the rocks? Perhaps he'd gotten disoriented.

"Tanner," she tried again, grabbing at his sleeve, but he put a finger to his lips and bent close until his mouth touched her cheek.

"Plan B." He kissed her before he drew away.

A kiss? It buzzed a warm electric spark on her cheek. She hadn't dreamed it. He had actually kissed her in the midst of the frightening chaos. Her heart pounded at the unexpected gesture. There was the tiniest quirk of a smile on his lips, though he seemed every bit intense and ready for an ambush. He extended his gloved hand to her.

Without hesitation, she took it. Did she trust him? She did. And she would follow no matter where he led her. It should have felt strange to abandon the guardedness that had been a hallmark of her life, yet it didn't. Natural, that's how it felt. As if she was following a path and a person God had provided just for her.

Mystified, she allowed him to guide her up, over the snow-covered granite humps. Britta kept pace as easily as if she was part mountain goat, but Mara's boots slipped and skidded on the frozen rock. When they got to a high point, the wind nearly flattened her. Backs pressed to the rock, Tanner pulled out the binoculars.

The seconds scrolled past, long and tense as he searched the terrain. "I don't see them."

"Do you think they went back for their snowmobiles?"

"That would be my guess. If they escaped the explosion, they probably split up. One after us on foot, the other returning for a machine."

Mara tried to get her bearings. "I can't acclimate. Where are we? Which direction is the campground and B and B?"

"That way," Tanner said, stabbing a finger northward. "But we're going to make a detour in the other direction. Climbing over the rocks was the fastest way to get back to where we need to be."

"A detour? Why?"

He didn't smile, but through the falling snow she thought she detected that mischievous gleam again. "Later, we'll talk. Now, we move."

Conversation ended, they climbed on.

Threading their way between the boulders, they climbed over a rocky ridge and down the other side. By the time they'd made it over the rock pile, she was winded, fingertips rubbed raw. Her boots punched into a patch of thigh-deep snow, instantly icing her lower limbs. Wriggling only served to sink her further. She was trapped in a snowy cocoon.

"Tanner…"

"Coming. Watch," he told his dog.

Britta scrambled up a fallen pine that had come to rest crookedly against another one. Nose quivering, she sampled the air.

He reached for Mara. "Hold on to me."

She grabbed his biceps and he extracted her from

the snow, hoisting her into his arms as if he was cradling a baby.

She hadn't time to even protest her awkward position as he carried her to the lower part of the pine, settling her on the trunk where he strapped on her snowshoes. She could do it herself, but with her fingers sore and freezing, it was better to let him. After hauling himself from the snow, he perched on the trunk next to her and tied on his own set. Again he took out the binoculars. "They won't suspect the route we've taken, but there's the chance they might have spotted us crossing the rocks. I don't see…"

Britta growled, low.

He jerked the lenses in the direction she was alerting. "Good girl, Britta." With one hand he stroked her ears. "I see him. It's Eli moving along the path heading away from the trailer."

Her stomach somersaulted. How could he still be in pursuit mode? Didn't the man ever slow? "Probably going for his machine?"

"No doubt."

Their window of escape was closing. Again. It was as though she was in the path of a relentless avalanche, no matter which way she turned or how fast she fled, Eli was there. And not just Eli. Vinny too. Tanner was right. The two men had split up. Vinny was tracking them on foot. Two enemies pinching in from different directions. *They'd be caught. Quickly.* She was almost too numb to feel the despair.

"The plan will still work. We'll head through the trees and backtrack to a spot about a quarter mile from the trailer."

She swallowed the tears. "But how is that going to help?" They should be heading away in the direction Britta had first led them. Tanner had already hopped down from the trunk. She had no choice but to do the same.

Tanner either hadn't heard her question or didn't want to answer. He had some scheme in mind and he was still confident it would work.

If he was confident, she would be too.

Praying his plan B would work, she pressed on after him.

Tanner wished they had time to shelter in place in the purple shadows of the pine forest, but he didn't dare. The winds might not be enough to completely obliterate their tracks and with Vinny no doubt on their tail, they didn't have much of a head start unless they'd managed to throw him off by climbing over the boulder pile. Vinny could be radioing information to Eli who would return as quickly as possible or circle around to cut them off once he figured out what Tanner was up to.

The branches absorbed some of the tumult while they moved parallel to the trailer again, which he knew was confusing Mara. She'd chosen to trust, instead of confronting him.

Lord, please help me make this work.

He didn't doubt that God heard his prayer, but he also knew God sometimes said no in heart-shattering ways, like He had with Allie. Tanner would never understand why she had to die, but he was coming to terms with the mystery of a God who both loved and said no. It could not be "no" this time, could it? A pointless question.

His duty was to struggle on with Mara, no matter how impossible the odds.

Deep in his bones he knew he wouldn't fail her, nor her brother, or Willow, Mara's father, all the people who were counting on him to bring her home. God would give him enough, moment by moment, perhaps, but it would be sufficient. He didn't know why it felt different than his bedside entreaties for Allie, but somehow it was.

They pushed on, stopping to check for signs of pursuit, wading along through the snow as if they were lumbering bears rudely awakened from their winter hibernation. Mara was dropping behind, fatigued. Britta looped back every few yards to encourage her with a tail wag or nose bump. Britta was tiring too, he could tell, and his own legs burned from the awkward waddling the snowshoes required. He decided he would up his gym quad workouts if he got back to Olympia.

Not if, *when*.

The hillocks of snow all began to look frighteningly familiar. Had he accidentally led them in a circle? Doubts swirled with the whirling bits of ice.

What if he couldn't find what he'd hidden? He remembered the utter vulnerability he'd felt that day when he'd been stranded on the glacier, cold, helpless to change his destiny. How small and insignificant, a puny flesh and blood man against the massive power of nature.

Same crushing wilderness, no help in sight, but he wasn't helpless now. Not even close. He had Britta and Mara and a lot more confidence in himself and the Lord. With gritted teeth he pulled out his phone and powered it on. By cupping his hands over the screen, he checked the GPS coordinates.

Correcting course, he led them to the hollow of three mighty oaks where the wind became more of a murmur than a scream. There, just under the snow-covered rock, was a corner of a blue tarp, lovelier than any sight he'd ever encountered. Relief warmed him from the inside out. He offered Mara a water bottle and drank from one himself before he filled his collapsible cup for Britta.

"All right. We can rest here for a few minutes before the next phase of plan B."

Mara wiped the water from her chapped lips. "Which is?"

He allowed himself a satisfied grin as he savored the green of her eyes and the sparkles that coated her lashes. "Why walk when you can ride?"

Her utter confusion made him laugh. "Did you call for a cab?" she quipped.

He picked up a corner of the tarp he'd buried and yanked it aside, revealing the snowmobile from the trailer. "Voila."

"Tanner! You're brilliant." She grabbed him in a hug that rocked him from side to side. His arms went around her, pulling her close, locking her next to his trip-hammering heart. He pressed his cold cheek against her head and her warmth eased into his frozen body. That kiss, the one he'd playfully pressed to her cheek, begged for a follow-up but it was enough simply to hold her close. He almost staggered when she let him go, staring at the machine.

"How in the world did you get it here?"

He chuckled. "Not so astonishing, really. While you

were showering and cooking, it occurred to me that having all our assets in one place put us at a disadvantage, so I filled up the tank, hoped the storm would muffle the noise and drove it out here. I covered the tarp with snow and stored the coordinates on my phone so I could find it again."

Her smile was more brilliant than sunlight on snow. "I am stunned by your cagey wilderness skills."

He bowed. "I aim to please." A clump of snow fell from overhead, startling them both, bringing them back to earth. "That's still the risk. Once we fire it up, if he's close, or Vinny is, they'll know our location immediately."

She shook her head. "They probably already do anyway."

"I'd originally thought we'd travel by night, but I don't think we can wait with Vinny behind us. Do you agree?"

"I do. I'm ready. Let's roll."

He quirked a brow. "Are you sure you're not justifying again because you're tired of snowshoeing hither and yon?"

Her grin lit up her face and his heart. "Hither is fine, it's the yon that's getting to me and besides, what could be better than you, me and Britta treating two killers to a taste of our exhaust?"

"I can't think of a single thing." He eyed the terrain. "You're absolutely positive? Once I turn on the engine, the cat's out of the bag." And the noise would paint an even bigger bullseye on their backs.

She reached for his hand. "Do we have time for a prayer?"

Her hand, offered to him, tore open something in his heart. He'd prayed relentlessly for Allie, yet it occurred to him that it was the very first time he would pray out loud with another woman. *Wrong, you can't pray with Mara.*

But his heart and soul disagreed with his brain. Slowly he took her hand. "Yes," he said around a clog in his throat. "Let's pray."

She did the talking and he mumbled a fervent "amen."

Less than a minute, but somehow it was perfect, humble gratitude, and faith-filled expectation. The tear inside him resettled itself and he had the strangest sensation of healing. In a daze, he climbed onto the driver's seat, and she seated herself behind him. Britta squeezed in the space between them. Removing the key from his pocket, he hesitated. The stakes were huge. There was no turning back.

He felt the pressure of his dog against his back and Mara's arms wrapped around his waist. Huge stakes indeed, he thought as he turned the key.

But the good guys were going to win this time.

EIGHT

The engine revved to life, echoing and bouncing through the trees like a struck gong. The noise twanged Mara's nerves as she clutched Tanner's sides, Britta lodged solidly between them. Tanner took it slow as they eased through the trees toward the clearing that they'd decided was the straightest route to take them to the bed-and-breakfast.

Though the machine rattled and shuddered her bones, Mara was relieved at not having to drag herself along at a snail's pace. If the fuel held out, she calculated they might be at the camp in a few hours. Her mind ran feverishly ahead. Maybe they wouldn't even need to stop at that midpoint. It was barely noon, they still had six hours of daylight to travel and depending on the terrain and fuel, they might even continue through the night as Tanner had originally planned. He had to be the cleverest man on the planet to think of hiding the snowmobile away from the trailer. She wished she had someone to tell, to brag about Tanner to.

He's not yours to brag about. She felt as if she should ease away, to mentally distance herself, but it took all her muscle power to clutch Tanner's waist both for her sake and Britta's. The snowmobile leaped and danced over hillocks as she tried to review how much food and water she'd packed before their hasty departure from the trailer.

Bang.

The sound was so unexpected, she could not place its origin. A broken branch? An engine malfunction?

Tanner shouted, something unintelligible. He jerked the handles sideways and she almost lost her grip. Britta yelped, slipping, but she pinned the dog with her weight to keep her from falling as Tanner hit the gas.

Another bang. Not a branch, a bullet. Her mouth went dry.

The report of the gun punched through the engine whine a third time. She tried to see the source but her hair covered her eyes and she didn't dare risk letting go to brush it away for fear she or Britta would tumble loose. As Tanner skidded the machine sideways, she got a glimpse of Vinny twenty yards away on cross-country skis, rifle raised and aimed for another shot.

Bang, bang. Two in quick succession. Tanner swerved in a tight turn, heading back for the cover of the trees. He looped from side to side as they raced on, trying to make them a harder target to hit, she realized. Mara clung tight until her fingers ached.

A bullet sizzled past her jacket. She curled lower, cradling Britta's body against her stomach. Only a few more feet to the trees. The sturdy trunks would protect them. Another shot pinged off the chassis of the snowmobile, shaving away bits of metal and plastic. Tanner swerved so abruptly, Mara screamed. He corrected and they flew toward the trees. Vinny shouted something, but Mara couldn't understand over the engine and her own thundering pulse.

The trees swam closer and closer, slashes of black against the dizzying white. If he lost control… Mara gritted her teeth. At the last possible moment, he accelerated and jerked right to keep them from smashing headfirst into a gnarled fir. She could feel his labored breathing as he slowed, moving them more cautiously through the trees, deeper into the comforting shadows. Vinny would be hard-pressed to follow on skis through the maze. With one hand, he reached behind to cup one of hers which was still clutching his jacket in a death grip. Britta snuffled Mara's neck as if to reassure her.

"You and Britta are still there? Unhurt?"

It required effort to force the words out. "Y-yes." She felt his sigh of relief. She shared the feeling, but her brain raced ahead to the next scenario. "We'll have to move slow, and Vinny will report to Eli."

"No choice," Tanner called over his shoulder. "The terrain here isn't optimal, but we'll make as much speed as we can."

They'd survived another death trap. *Thank You, Lord.* She rested her forehead between his shoulder blades, earning a chin lick from Britta. Leaning on his shoulders was comforting and she could not resist giving him a squeeze and whispering in his ear. "Thank you for getting us out of there."

He shifted. Uncomfortable at the intimacy? He didn't need her for comfort, she realized, but the reverse was becoming a problem. She leaned back a fraction. There was work to be done if they were going to make it, she chided herself. "I can help with the landmarks if my childhood memories hold up. As soon as my brain starts to cooperate again, I mean."

"I know where north is so that's enough for now."

He began to weave through the trees. She tried to ease her grip, but the route was rough as Tanner avoided buried rocks and branches that could wreck the machine or eject them for sure. They soldiered on for what had to be close to an hour, judging by the weak glimpses of sky she spied through the tree branches and storm clouds. They stopped periodically, turning off the engine to listen for indications of Eli or Vinny's approach. Each pause made her insides quiver, waiting for the sound of death approaching, but they heard nothing.

Another hour of riding and her legs were cramping and the small of her back spasmed. Britta wriggled.

"I think Britta needs to get down for a minute," she called in Tanner's ear. He pulled to a stop at the base of an ancient redwood and killed the engine.

Britta scrambled loose and immediately stretched from tail to ears.

Mara heaved her leg over the side and hopped off into the snow. Her muscles screamed in protest. "Feels like we've been through the washing machine."

Tanner did the same, bending over, hands on his knees. Probably exhausted both mentally and physically like she was.

Massaging her arms she attempted to restore circulation. "I…" She stopped, shocked as she saw the blood. It smeared her wrist and up along her forearm. Had she been struck? But there was no pain, no rip in her jacket sleeve. After a long drawn-out moment, she realized it was not her blood she was looking at. In horror, her gaze traveled to Tanner. "You're bleeding."

He looked down at the tear in his jacket, not surprised or upset. "Yeah," he said with a sigh. "Plan B didn't exactly go off without a hitch, did it?"

Tanner had known he'd been struck by something, maybe a piece ricocheting off the snow machine, but it hadn't felt like a major injury and there was no way he was going to stop and take a look until he got them far away from Vinny. Now he realized there was more blood than he'd thought, though the pain was only a dull throb courtesy of the frigid temperatures numbing his nerves. At least the cold was good for something.

Mara alternated between raging and silence.

"You knew you'd been hit and we didn't stop? All this way and you didn't so much as hint about an injury?" She tugged him to a flat rock where she dusted off the snow and forced him to sit, none too gently.

"It's…"

She stabbed a pointer finger at him. "If you tell me it's nothing to worry about, I will refuse to speak to you for the rest of the trip, Tanner Ford. It will be a silent treatment unlike any you've ever experienced."

That made him both smile and close his mouth as she unzipped his backpack and rummaged for his standard issue first aid kit. The cold air made him gasp as she peeled up his shirt to expose his ribs. Britta raced to his side, investigating the source of his discomfiture. The wound was maybe four inches long, a gash that probably would require stitches in other circumstances.

He patted the dog. "See? Not life-threatening."

She glared. "That's the same as saying it's nothing to worry about. Again, dangerously close to earning yourself the silent treatment." She cleaned her hands, pulled on a pair of plastic gloves and ripped opened the sterile packages. Britta whined and tried to climb in his lap. Mara eased her away. "Don't worry, Britta. I got this. It's a job that requires fingers not paws."

She applied a disinfectant which stung enough to make his eyes water though he didn't cry out. "You sure you're qualified?" he teased through gritted teeth.

She didn't smile, but her frown eased somewhat. "My dad worked on an ambulance when he was young so he taught me about first aid. Every doll and teddy bear in my room sported some sort of bandage or sling."

"Did you lose any patients, Doctor Mara?"

She didn't miss a beat. "Only the bunny and that was because the dog chewed her up."

Britta's head cocked at the word dog. Mara's tiny sliver of a grin made him realize he was forgiven, mostly. He figured he'd test the waters. "When Britta was a puppy she used to whine at night so I gave her a catcher's mitt because I didn't have any stuffed animals. She still sleeps with Mitt when we're home."

Mara laughed. "Don't worry, Britta. I'll get you a proper dog toy when we get back."

When they got back... It hit him then. What would there be between him and Mara when they returned to Olympia? But he knew already...they'd be colleagues, friends maybe, separated by that comfortable space that kept him afloat. *Treading water, like he'd been doing for four years.* A cloud settled over his heart. She snapped him out of his thoughts by smoothing on the bandage and pulling his shirt back into place, followed by the jacket.

She stowed the trash in a zippered pocket. "All right. Good as I can do for now. We'll need to check soon and see if you've saturated the bandage."

"I'll try not to."

"And I'll drive for a while to spare you the movement."

"I…"

She raised a finger again and he quieted under the ferocity of that gaze. "This is how it's going to be. Snow's falling harder now. I recognize that ridge of rock in the distance. We're close to the camp, and I think I can get us there. I can drive a snowmobile as well as you can."

He zipped his jacket, the chill penetrating his body down to the cellular level, but he was determined not to shiver in front of her. "Stopping is risky. We need to keep going, try and make the bed-and-breakfast."

"Not with you losing blood. You need rest, food and water. And that's exactly what you would tell me if I was injured so don't bother arguing."

He closed his mouth, the response dying on his lips. She was right. It was precisely what he'd have advised, insisted on, demanded even.

She got up and stood there, hands on hips. "Ready to move out?"

Against the pewter sky, her expression shone with determination and toughness. Yet he'd been privileged to have seen her tender side, her humor, her humility. He marveled at this woman who'd lived through a maelstrom and stood strong as the ancient trees behind her… *He shall strengthen thy heart*… The snippet came to him unbidden. Like Allie, she was her own woman, strong enough to march steadily forward no matter what came at her, to live her life on her own terms and accept the growth that came with the struggle. Her strength chimed a note inside he had not heard for years. Mara was ready to tackle the next challenge.

What about you, Tanner?

A falling twig broke his reverie. Here, in the forest, wounded and on the run was not the time to reevaluate. Whatever he was daydreaming about had to be brought to heel and quickly. Mara was not Allie, she was a protectee and right now, she was protecting him which was a maddening situation that could not be allowed to continue. The wolves were circling, and their little trio was alone in a great big wilderness. He got to his feet, hiding a grimace of pain. "How far do you figure to the camp?"

"At our speed, a couple of hours, maybe." She climbed onto the driver's seat. He slid on behind her, making room for Britta between them. The dog's bony flank pressed against his ribs, compressing the bandage against the wound.

He clenched his jaw. Pain wasn't a bad thing if it would keep him focused. At least he could keep watch for Eli and Vinny as Mara concentrated on driving. It took her only a few awkward lurches to get comfortable with piloting the snowmobile. Asher had told him one of the few positive memories he'd had of his father was snowmobiling. He'd heard Mara describing snowmobiling with their dad, as well. Strange how Mara's father had cut himself off from Asher for years, embracing only his second family with Mara and her mother until God convinced him to make amends. His decision had kept the siblings apart, sealed off from each other when they could have been a source of support and love. Again, he wondered why his mind was spinning off into such deep philosophical places. The injury maybe, drawing energy away from his faculties where he really needed it.

The cold intensified along with the storm as the afternoon wore into evening. His wound ignited at each bump they encountered. The terrain had grown steeper, their progress sloughing off shelves of snow that disappeared behind them. The "couple of hours" stretched much longer as they had to circle around unstable areas and slopes that were too steep to tackle. When there was barely enough light to illuminate their path, he touched her shoulder, calling over the noise. "Too dark. Getting dangerous. We have to stop."

"We're almost there. I know it. Two more minutes."

Two minutes spooled into five. "Mara, we have to find shelter."

"Wait."

The cold and his pain left his patience in tatters. He'd yank the key from the ignition if he had to. "No more. Time to stop."

She eased the machine at the top of the ridge and over, halting so abruptly his ribs ached. Had she heard Vinny? Eli? He put a hand on his weapon and craned his neck.

"It's camp." She pointed.

He strained to see as she crested the high point and drove onto a heavily wooded plateau. It looked nothing like a camp in the dim light, until his eyes adjusted enough to pick out three platform tents protruding above the snow line, two with gaping holes in the canvas. The third appeared relatively intact. There were the ruins of a wooden structure nearby. He could hardly believe what he was seeing. Shelter. This oasis had no palm trees and balmy weather, but it would be a lifesaver nonetheless.

Without a word she drove straight for the most intact of the three tents and parked the snowmobile around the back. He helped cut down some pine branches which would at least screen it from view if someone didn't look too carefully. Hopefully their tracks would be sufficiently blurred by the next wave of snowfall.

Mara flashed a weary smile. "How about we take the best room? Four-star accommodations, all the way."

"It's all going to be four stars if we can get out of this storm." He stopped talking as Britta sniffed and circled the tent. Her body went stiff.

He unsnapped his revolver.

Mara shook her head, mouth slack. "Eli couldn't be here. There's no possible way."

Not likely, certainly, but he wouldn't put anything past the man. Eli had promised he would kill to prevent Mara testifying and he'd meant every last syllable. "We'll check. One second."

He eased up the wooden step, avoiding a rotted board.

Britta was excited, twitchy, not her usual on-duty behavior. "What's inside, girl?" he whispered.

She flapped her ears. Not Eli. Britta would have signaled with a sit. Then who? What? Something rustled inside. He crouched low and unzipped the tent flap, turning on his light. Britta barked, tail wagging. Not a human…

He hadn't finished the thought when his flashlight picked up a set of yellow eyes. Britta yowled and he was so relieved he forgot to give her a stay command. Taking advantage, she jetted inside, barking at the cornered raccoon who hissed with jaws open and sharp white teeth on display.

"Leave it," he finally managed, after holstering his gun. Britta obediently scooted backward and sat, but her ears were still twitching at the masked rodent which was now scurrying through a hole in the warped floor.

With a sigh, he stuck his head out. "Britta has secured us a tent, but the evicted raccoon is disgruntled, to say the least."

Grinning, she handed him his backpack and carried the other one inside with her. "I guess it'll be putting up a bad review for this establishment. I've had a few encounters with raccoons lately. There's a reason they wear masks. Very untrustworthy." Once inside, she zipped the canvas flaps closed. "Not the Ritz, but better than nothing."

"Much better." The interior was excruciatingly cold, but the old canvas kept the wind and snow at bay. There were four wooden bed frames with no bedding or mattresses, a small freestanding cupboard and a set of crooked bookshelves covered with mold. He strode to the cupboard and picked it up, ignoring his complaining ribs.

She hurried to help him. "What are you doing? You're going to reopen that wound."

"Gotta put out the no vacancy sign for the rodents." Together they dragged the cupboard to block up the hole where the raccoon had disappeared.

They were actively shivering, but there was nothing to be done about that. He settled onto one of the planked beds and she sat cross-legged on the other, rummaging in her pack. He produced a bowl of kibble and water for Britta, spilling some when his frozen fingers refused to cooperate.

Britta ate a few half-hearted bites before she quit.

He got out the two silver emergency blankets and handed one to Mara.

"Later," she said. "I want to check your wound."

This time he didn't argue. She lifted his jacket and shirt and peered at the bandage. "Good. No saturation. I think we can leave it for now."

He sighed, hauling himself to his feet, ignoring her protest. "Gonna check." He went to the tent flap and stepped out on the landing, scanning through his night vision binoculars in all directions through the howling wind. When he returned, his cheeks burned and his eyes watered. He could not control the shuddering of his limbs. She handed him a tin cup.

His senses worked overtime to process. Warmth seeped through the metal into his numb fingertips. The scent of cinnamon and orange tea tickled his nostrils. He gaped at her. "Hot tea? How did you…?"

"If you can produce a snowmobile, I can rummage up some tea." She laughed at his surprise and poured a cup for herself. "Told you this was a four-star accommodation. I bought a thermos in a secondhand shop along with this jacket. Fugitive life lesson. When I went on the run, I learned that some hotels and gas stations had complimentary coffee stations. Anytime I could find one I'd help myself to coffee and fill my thermos for later. After I boiled water this morning, I filled it and added a tea bag before Eli ambushed us at the trailer. I figured anything warm would be a bonus."

He stared, letting the precious warmth seep into his body. "Mara, you are incredible."

She pinked. "Just trying to keep up. If you think the tea is good, you're really going to love this."

Right before his eyes she withdrew a black pouch from her backpack and produced a tiny butane-powered camping burner. "I must be hallucinating."

"No, you're not. I found it in the trailer and I packed it." She carried the contraption near one of the closed window flaps and set it up on the bookcase before she unzipped the flap to allow for ventilation. "Bummer to let the cold air in, but I don't see how it could get much chillier in here."

"For warm food, I'd say it's worth it."

"Can't really cook too well, but we can heat up stuff, right?" While he sipped from his precious cup of tea, she set about popping the lid off a tomato soup can and setting it on the burner. On top of that, she carefully balanced a pile of pancakes.

Tea? Pancakes? A burner? What else could this woman come up with?

She pressed close to the glow of the burner and gestured him to join her. "I don't know how much butane is left so we'd better get lots of bang for our buck."

Agog, he joined her. They crowded shoulder to shoulder to soak in the meager warmth from the minuscule burner, savoring the smell of the tomato soup and pancakes.

She sighed. "I never really appreciated the comforts

I had before, all the freedoms and the luxuries until they were taken away. Something as simple as clean, dry socks. I never paid a bit of mind to having them at my fingertips. Now I do." Her eyes filled with tears.

He wrapped an arm around her shoulders and pulled her to him.

Me too. Gratitude filled his every atom, for the spot of warmth, their momentary safety, Mara's resourcefulness. He felt in that moment a rush of emotion he could not fully explain. A profound gratitude that he was standing with this woman, in a barren tent, surrounded by a raging storm, more appreciative than he'd ever been in his entire three plus decades.

With Mara? Not Allie? Guilt washed over him, but not strong enough to knock out the strange peace. They stood together, admiring the little blue flame until the soup was bubbling hot and the pancakes were warm to the touch. He finished his tea and she refilled the cup with soup.

She turned off the burner, rezipped the window flap and they carried their feast to the bed platforms. Not as limber as she, he couldn't sit cross-legged, so he balanced the pancakes on one knee and held the tin cup in the other.

He gave Britta one of the pancakes. In a fit of canine delight, she licked it thoroughly before she devoured it in two bites. He poured a bit of the warmed soup in his palm for her. Britta didn't care that it wasn't standard dog supplies. She licked it up in a flash.

"That will warm up your tummy, Boo Bear." He was pleased that she returned to her kibble and finished that too.

Mara chuckled. "So happy to see her gobble up her food. It reminds me of the bloodhound puppies. How are they?"

"They've had a tumultuous puppyhood." He explained that the bloodhounds, gifted to the PNK9, had gone missing for months after being stolen from the facility where they were being trained.

Her eyes flew wide. "Unbelievable. And they were all recovered? How are they?"

"I can give you a good report. Asher and Peyton recovered them. They were being used by a drug runner to find his missing cocaine shipment. All three of those saggy, baggy bloodhounds have been brought back to the unit in good health. They're being assessed, but hopefully they can be trained out of whatever problems they have and serve on the team."

She sighed. "I forget time has passed. They aren't roly-poly puppies anymore. They're on their way to being two-year-olds by now. And the PNK9 candidates? Are Veronica, Parker, Owen and Brandie still competing for jobs? Was there any decision on that?"

"Turns out Owen was trying to sabotage the others, even pushed Brandie in the path of a van full of tourists. He was dismissed and might be facing charges."

She goggled. "You have got to be kidding me."

"No, ma'am. I kid you not. There had been no decision when I left to find you on which of the three will get the two jobs."

"I can hardly believe it. So much has changed. And I thought we were the ones going through the storm." She cupped her palms around the warm soup and sighed.

"That's the name of the game, isn't it? To find contentment in the midst of it all."

He nodded. "Sounds so easy."

"And yet it's not." She put her cup down. "Would you say grace?"

"I'd be honored." He said a heartfelt thank-you to the Lord for the food, for their survival and for the contentment they'd found together in the midst of a storm. When he'd finished, he locked eyes with her.

Why is it that I feel content right now? And how will I feel when we return to civilization?

NINE

Mara drained every drop of her tomato soup, sopping up the remnants with a pancake. Tanner did the same, and his delight warmed her soul. The food combination would have been strange in every other circumstance, but for that moment, it was manna. God had provided. Again.

When the meal was done, she wiped the tin cups with a paper towel she'd packed and used the clean cups to heat some of the bottled water, refilling the thermos and stowing it in the backpack. She wondered if she'd ever unlearn the habit. When the stove was cool she packed that too. Since she was wearing every item of clothing she'd brought including her pink hat, there was nothing else left to tidy up. She and the backpack would be ready to flee with Tanner and Britta in seconds if their attackers returned, but it would take a minute to climb aboard the snowmobile, start the engine, assess the storm-ravaged terrain. Would seconds be enough if Eli found them?

Cleanup complete, they wrapped themselves in the silver blankets as the temperatures continued to drop. Even with all the tent flaps zipped tight, frigid air seeped up from cracks between the wooden floorboards. All three of them shivered uncontrollably.

"D-do you think Eli will track us here?" Her breath puffed a white cloud into the air.

"No, but I'm going to scan every couple hours. Hoping we can ship out before dawn. As soon as there's a break in the storm, we need to make tracks for the B and B. I'll wake you when conditions look acceptable."

"Let me help keep watch. I can do a shift."

This time Tanner held up a finger. "I'm rested, I've been fed and my wound is healing as well as can be expected. My watch. No arguments."

She was too cold to put up a fuss anyway. Cocooned in her silver blanket like a human baked potato, she rolled into a ball on the hard wood support, ruing the missing mattress. Like countless nights over the past seven months, the frigid conditions seemed to worsen with every passing moment. There had been some endless, lonely hours when she'd wondered if the morning would ever come, or if she would live to see it. But this time, she was not alone. Her shivers intensified. She barely felt the tap on her shoulder.

"Britta needs a pal." She lifted her arm and Britta burrowed in next to her. The warmth of that furry body touching hers was exquisite. Britta pressed her cold nose to Mara's chin and she scrubbed the dog's neck gratefully. He draped the second silver blanket over them.

"Don't you need…?" she started.

"Get some sleep." Tanner's tone was almost curt so she decided not to press. With her warm companion, her misery subsided enough that she drifted off.

Hours later she heard Tanner get up from his bed

and felt the blast of air from the tent flap opening. He could not hide the violent chattering of his teeth when he returned.

"Tanner?"

"A-all c-c-clear."

"You're frozen. Take one of these silver blankets."

"No, you…"

"It's too cold. No arguments."

After a long moment, he accepted. The silver crackled as his body tremored with cold from the opposite bed.

Gradually, Tanner's shivering eased off and Britta's throaty snore filled the space between them. It was still brutally cold, but her relief that Tanner wasn't going to get frostbite or hypothermia allowed her to doze.

Over the next few hours she was vaguely aware that he'd risen again, twice more. The last time, she'd dozed, until he grasped her shoulder. Britta was already up, lapping water, wearing her snow booties.

Mara rubbed her eyes. "Danger?"

"No. Opportunity. Storm's slackened."

"What time is it?"

"Almost four."

"Do we have time to eat?"

"Something cold."

"No problem there. Everything's cold." Each joint and muscle screamed in discomfort as she clambered off her wooden bed. Never again would she take a mattress for granted. Forcing her numb fingers to perform, she fished through her pack and pulled out the jar of peanut butter and one of jelly, along with a sleeve of crackers. With a plastic knife she quickly made up three peanut butter and jelly cracker sandwiches for each of them and one for Britta. Using the instant coffee and a half cup of lukewarm water each, she prepared them a beverage.

He drained the coffee in three swallows. "Fantastic."

"Wish we could warm more water to refill my thermos."

She saw by the tense twitch of his mouth that wasn't going to happen, so she drank her coffee and packed their cups.

Tanner dragged the cupboard they'd used to cover the raccoon hole back to its original position.

She cocked a brow at him, puzzled. "Are you afraid the establishment won't like us leaving the furniture askew?"

He shrugged. "I figured the raccoon deserves to reclaim his space. Nothing should be out in this cold for long without shelter."

A spot of warmth kindled in her heart. Tanner was a kind man, through and through. She presented him with his stack of crackers and one for Britta.

The dog lashed her tail in anticipation before Tanner gave her the cracker snack.

"She's going to expect treats like this from now on." His words were light, but she could hear the stress threaded underneath. In the glow of the tiny flashlight he'd activated, she caught the purple shadows of exhaustion under his eyes. He'd been up all night, freezing and in pain, trying to spot Eli in the tumult, the burden of the protector.

"I'll drive," she said quickly.

"We'll split it. I'll take the first leg. Ready?"

"After we change your bandage."

This time he didn't even sigh, simply unzipped his

jacket and let her change out the dressing for a fresh one. Again there was no saturation and the wound looked no worse than the previous day. She tore off a length of medical tape and affixed the fresh pad. "You're worried."

"I'd feel a ton better if I could send a text or call Asher and the team. At least give them our location. Can't get a single bar. It's like we've been thrown down a well or something."

"As soon as we get to the inn, we can get word out."

He didn't reply, but she knew what he was thinking. *It's a long way between here and there.*

"We'll make it." Before she could second-guess herself she pressed her hand to his face and kissed him softly. His lips were warm, scented with peanut butter. He cupped her palm against his cheek looking into her eyes with an expression she could not decipher. Was it wonder? Confusion? Longing? Maybe she was projecting her own feelings onto him.

He blinked and moved his hand away.

Recrimination flooded in. *You were wrong to kiss him.*

But it was just out of gratitude, not any other reason, she told herself.

Then why was that kiss looping warm circles through her body? And why did her stomach drop when he'd moved away?

"All set," she said, only a touch breathlessly. "Locked and loaded, as you cops say."

"Yes. Last leg. Ready to get this over with?"

The journey? Yes. Her time with Tanner? On that subject she wasn't nearly as certain. Fortunately, he hadn't waited for a reply. He was already unzipping the tent flap with Britta by his side, letting in a blast of biting air.

It was very clear that he was itching to finish his mission.

Ready to deliver her back to her life.

And him to his.

So get used to the idea. Your hours with Tanner are numbered.

But she knew she'd never forget the time in that freezing tent, fighting to keep one another alive, joined at a level they'd never experienced before. She'd always have that memory, no matter what happened.

With one last glance back at the empty tent, she plunged out into the cold.

Tanner felt each bump and dip in his aching bones as they eased their way into the trees. The weather had settled into a soft curtain of snow, still substantial, but the winds had died away. Easier to drive.

Easier for Eli to track them.

Comforting to have Britta and Mara sandwiched behind him, but disconcerting to remember how he'd felt in the wake of Mara's kiss. It was as though all the knots holding him together had come loose at once, his heart, his mind, his emotions, unmoored.

He'd felt that only once before, when Allie died, and he'd promised himself—no vowed—that he would never allow himself to experience such profound rattling again. The love of his life was dead. He would go on without her until he was too. End of story.

But suddenly he was awash in the same feelings of

uncertainty, lashes of joy in between waves of fear and worry.

Mara's kiss…

He gripped the handles tighter and willed away the thoughts as the canopy above them thickened and the way became pitched upward.

"We're close," Mara said in his ear. "There's a trail-head another half mile from here."

He motored on, the tickle of unease over Eli's where-abouts turning into a small stream. Eli would have to know they'd head for help, any kind of help. And the only thing for twenty square miles other than hunting and fishing cabins was the Rainier Hike-Inn. It was possible Eli didn't know about the place if he hadn't grown up in the area, but the guy was a whiz at find-ing information. Not that hard to ask a local or search it online if he could get onto the internet.

They found the trailhead, marked by a pile of stones mostly buried in snow. The top stone was engraved with Rainier-Hike Inn, 11 miles. Engine idling he stared up the narrow path barely demarcated by wooden arrows nailed into the trunks of the pines.

"Uphill, huh? No way the snowmobile can take that grade."

Mara sighed. "But there's a downhill to every uphill, as Dad used to say." He heard the catch in her voice as she climbed off, Britta beside her.

"You okay?"

She nodded. "Reminds me of better days for Dad. I've worried about how much he's slipped while I've been gone. What did he think happened to me? Did they tell him anything?"

"I'm not sure. I never asked Asher."

She passed a hand over her forehead. "And the thing that really scares me. Will he recognize me when I get back?"

He squeezed her hand. "You can tell him stories. Remind him. He'll probably be pretty excited to know you revisited the campsite he used to take you to."

She nodded, as if trying to convince herself. "I'll tell him when we get back."

Together they pushed the snowmobile behind a clump of rocks and strapped on their snowshoes. He offered to take her pack.

"No. It's lighter now that we drank the soup. Box of raisins before we hike?"

He didn't want to take the time, but his stomach was hollowed out with hunger. They shared the last of the warm water and gave some to Britta, along with some dog treats. The raisins were gloriously sweet, plump in his mouth. "Never really appreciated a raisin before."

"Me neither, but being a fugitive makes you enjoy all kinds of things that way."

Packs in place, they began the arduous uphill trek. His thighs were burning after only a dozen strides. It was necessary to stop and catch their breath every fifteen minutes. He could hardly believe it was only eleven o'clock when he checked his watch as they tackled mile three. It felt as though they'd been traveling forever. The trail peaked and shifted into a looping path that was easier to navigate but less direct. Noon crept to one, two and almost to three o'clock before they spotted the roof of the log-sided structure. It was shrouded in white, but the tiniest curl of smoke emanated from the brick chimney. He rubbed his eyes to be sure he wasn't dreaming.

The lodge really was standing there sturdy and solid, and obviously with a fire burning inside. Food, warmth, communication...a generator. Were they really so close to rescue? Finally eluding the threat that had dogged Mara since April? She was moving faster now, her face shining with hope that weakened his knees.

Britta too had a spring in her step as they clomped along the last stretch of the trail. All he needed was a working phone or enough of a signal to make the call himself.

He stopped on the porch, removed his police jacket and took off Britta's official harness.

Mara gave him a quizzical brow.

"I want to get the lay of the land before we tell anybody our story."

They removed their snowshoes and pushed open the heavy wooden door, greeted by a cozy paneled room with a blazing fire and sturdy wood furniture clustered around a braided rug. A desk cluttered with papers, file folders and three empty coffee mugs occupied the corner. A baseball bat was perched in the corner. *For sport or protection?*

Mara almost ran to the fireplace, yanking off her gloves and shoving her fingers nearly to the metal screen. Tanner hurried to the desk with Britta at his side.

"Hello? Is anyone here?"

After several moments a middle-aged man with a drooping mustache appeared, a mug wrapped in his palm. "Oh, hey. Thought I was hearing things. Didn't expect anyone to hike up here with our current weather situation." He blinked at Mara and Britta through horn-rimmed glasses. "Name's Pete."

"Tanner, and this is Mara and my dog, Britta."

He smiled. "Good thing we're a pet-friendly establishment."

Tanner had no time for chitchat. "Can I use your phone?"

"Aww, man, normally I'd say yes in a heartbeat, but everything's knocked down. Only got enough juice from the generator to run the heat and lights upstairs and the bottom floor rooms have no power at all. Fortunately, there's only one other couple here right now."

"How about email?"

"Sorry. Computer service is out too and most people can't text here even when we don't have a blizzard. Storm should blow over in the next few days and they'll get the cell tower fixed. In the meantime…" He shrugged.

Tanner felt his stomach contract to the size of a fist. No communication with Asher. Too risky to keep traveling. Had they moved from one vulnerable spot to another?

Mara was at his side now. "What about rooms? Two?"

Tanner felt the man's eyes wander over him and then consider Mara. He wondered if he should reveal he was a cop, but he didn't know how discreet Pete actually was. If Eli or Vinny did track them, who was to say that Pete wouldn't take a bribe to rat them out? It was a possibility that Eli had already paid a visit to the lodge and coerced Pete to alert him if they arrived? Best not to take chances. "Two rooms," he repeated. "For me and my cousin."

"I can give you a couple upstairs that adjoin. Ground

floor's got no power except for the dining room like I said. I live here but my staff has to hike in and out so they're all stranded at home. Thus there's no maid or laundry service. I can offer snacks until they run out and a simple meal zapped in the microwave by yours truly, but that's about it for amenities."

"If the rooms are warm and there's hot coffee, that's more than plenty." Mara gave him her thousand-watt smile.

He tipped his mug at her. "Right through that doorway is the dining room and there's a fresh pot of coffee. I'll get your keys and bring them to you." He raised an eyebrow. "After we take care of the payment."

Tanner blinked. They'd been so far removed from the real world he'd forgotten how things were done. He handed over his credit card.

"Tanner Ford," the clerk said, reading the card. He looked at Mara. "And your last name?"

"Smith," Tanner supplied. "Go on through and get yourself some coffee," he told her. "Pour some for me too, okay?"

Mara understood. Pete wasn't to be trusted. She nodded and left.

"So," Pete said as he gave Tanner a bill to sign. "Where'd you folks hike in from?"

"You know what, Pete?" Tanner said with a warm smile, "I'm so bushed I can hardly stand. Gotta get my dog some water and thaw out. I'll fill you in soon, okay?"

Pete capped the ballpoint pen. "Sure thing. Chat later."

But Pete knew Tanner had avoided the question. He could feel the clerk's eyes following him and Britta as they went to find Mara. Suspicion prickled his skin. Was Pete an enemy or friend? They'd likely have to wait a few more days to establish contact with the PNK9 team.

In forty-eight hours, who knew what could happen?

They might have found respite from the storm, but they were still a long way from home.

TEN

Mara drank a second cup of decaf so fast it burned her mouth. Warmth, fluids, walls. Her brain simply would not believe that she was standing inside a building with heat and running water. And a bathroom, probably many of them, she thought with a thrill. It was like being a castaway finally brought aboard a rescue ship. Tanner refused a cup and ushered her upstairs to the rooms they'd been assigned.

Unlocking the door with an old-fashioned key, he stopped her on the threshold, pulled the scent article from Eli and let Britta have a sniff to remind her. He wished he had something of Vinny's to offer the dog. Britta checked the tiny room, under the full bed with its patchwork quilt, the tiny closet and cramped bathroom. All clear.

"You don't trust Pete," she said when he and Britta returned.

"I don't know him, but I know Eli and he'll grease any palm or threaten anyone to get what he wants. Look what happened with Howard at the gas station."

"But if you told Pete you're a cop…"

"Mara, we're trapped here until we get help or hike out.

There's no one around for miles to come to our rescue and I can't assume people have good intentions."

She sank down on the bed. "You're right, and I know I should be worried sick, but honestly, I can't quite suppress the thrill of sitting on an honest-to-goodness mattress."

He smiled at her, the expression easing the tension from his bruised and battered face.

"I should check your bandage."

"Not necessary. I'll check it myself. Why don't you get some sleep and we'll meet up again in a couple of hours? My room's right next door, but I think Britta should stay with you. If you don't mind, we can leave the adjoining door unlocked tonight."

"I don't mind." Actually it was a huge relief, though she didn't say so. And why didn't she? Why did she feel suddenly shy around Tanner now that they were temporarily not fighting for their lives? "But before nap there's a bath with my name on it. And would you look at that fluffy bath towel hanging on the shower bar? It's a work of art."

He laughed and turned to Britta. "Watch."

Britta sat at attention.

"If Eli approaches, she'll bark. I'll hear. I think she'll alert to Vinny's presence as well, but lock the door though, anyway?"

"What are you going to do while I'm on this mini vacation?"

"Take advantage of the fact that Vinny and Eli aren't here, yet."

Yet. That one syllable brought her bumping back to the hard ground.

"I'll stay on this floor while Britta's on watch. Gonna prowl around and try to send a text. Maybe I'll be the one in a million that gets a message out."

You're already one in a million. Mara closed the door and locked it. In the bathroom she did the same, though she knew Britta was a champion alert dog. She carefully removed her father's banged-up watch. She pictured him the last time she'd seen him, thin in the beloved yellow sweater she'd gifted him when she'd taken the picture for her keychain.

"*Who are you?*" Three words that pierced her heart like arrows.

"*Mara,*" she'd reminded him. "*I'm Mara, your daughter.*"

"*I thought I had a son.*"

"*You do. His name is Asher. He's my brother.*"

"*Will he come to see me too?*"

Her heart cracked wider then, opening up the fissure that had started the day she'd learned of his diagnosis. His memory seemed to be receding by inches, the confusion eating away the more recent memories first and burrowing backward in time. How long would it be before he didn't remember her at all? "*I'm sure he will, Dad. Soon.*"

But Asher had only made a cursory visit to the facility where their dad lived. He'd not yet let go the hurt from their father's betrayal, though she'd prayed for that very thing for years. The burden was a rock pile between her and Asher too. *That doesn't matter now.* She turned the taps to extra hot. *You're going back home and you'll try again with Asher.* Dad would be safe and maybe he really would receive a meaningful visit from his son.

Submerged in the water up to her chin, she thanked God for their respite. Tears spilled down her face into the bathwater. A tub was another item added to her "never to be taken for granted again" list. She shampooed her hair twice and scrubbed her skin, gently over the bruises and banged spots. Her shin sported a long yellowing bruise. How lovely it was to be warm. Had it been only twelve hours before that she and Tanner had survived a bitterly cold night in a ramshackle tent cabin? But God had given them the strength to get through it...together.

The together part was temporary, she reminded herself, using another of the tiny bars of soap the lodge provided, inhaling the faint vanilla scent. Though the old cast iron tub kept the water hot, she could not completely force away the nagging chill of danger.

It worried Tanner that there had been no sign of Eli on the last leg of their trip from the campsite. Was it possible he'd fled? Decided to skip the country to avoid being arrested and brought to trial for murdering Jonas and Stacey? With the storm passed, the roads would open up sooner or later and communication would be restored. Perhaps Eli and Vinny had given up. She wanted to believe it, but she couldn't make herself.

When she was good and pruney, she forced herself out of the tub and into her grimy clothes. She hoped there would be some garments she could borrow or buy. A tacky sweatshirt with the lodge's name on it maybe? Her jeans were torn at the knee and the jacket was covered with smears of pitch. Towel drying her hair left it in tousled kinks which she pulled back with a rubber band. Her stomach growled and she remembered Pete had said something about snacks. Britta wagged her tail approvingly as if she'd read Mara's mind about the food idea.

She tapped on their adjoining door and Tanner opened instantly. "What's wrong?"

She held up her palms. "Nothing but I'm too hungry to nap."

He exhaled. "I'm hungry too, but I didn't want to rifle through your backpack or crack open an MRE. Dining room?"

"Dining room."

As he let her pass him as they entered the hallway, she heard him inhale.

"Are you sniffing me, Officer Tanner?"

He turned a shade of scarlet. "Uh, ah, I mean… actually…" He exhaled. "Yes. You smell nice, like a cupcake."

She giggled. "Thank you. The perfume is courtesy of the Rainier Hike-Inn soap."

"Works on you."

The three made their way down the creaking staircase to the dining room. A woman with a wild mop of white hair greeted them, a Danish in her hand. "Hi. I'm Ellen and this is my husband George. You must be the new arrivals."

The bearded man was peering into a cupboard. He waved at them.

"He's tired of eating Danish, so he's looking for fruit or something. I'm perfectly happy with frosting and pastry. Here." She pushed a plate at them.

"Thanks. I'm Mara and this is my…uh, cousin Tanner."

She arched her brow. "Happy to meet you and your cousin and your dog."

Britta wagged her tail but did not approach the woman.

Mara tried to keep up the stream of conversation, but after she unwrapped the Danish she was so hungry she'd devoured the whole thing without saying a word.

Ellen flashed her a surprised smile and pushed the pastry basket closer. "Wow. You must have had a hard journey to get here. Have another."

You don't know the half of it. "We had some transportation troubles and got stuck in the storm. I sure could use a change of clothes. Is there a gift shop here?"

Ellen laughed. "It's not that fancy a place, but there is a room where Pete keeps a bunch of lost and found stuff and there are clothes in there. I know because I was trying to find my missing scarf. Didn't find it, but there was another one and Pete said everything's up for grabs. His housekeeper launders everything before it gets stowed away so theoretically it's clean too."

"Super." Mara reached for another Danish and handed one to Tanner as he slid two cups of coffee in front of them. She tried to keep the expression of sheer bliss under control. They were supposed to be traveling cousins, not starving fugitives on the run from a killer.

"Have you gotten any signal for your phone?" Tanner took an enormous bite.

George plopped down and peeled an overripe banana. "Nah. I was trying to find a spot today too. Think I've scoped out every room on the ground floor. The inn's mostly a dead zone, says Pete, but I'm not giving up."

Ellen rolled her eyes. "How did we possibly survive before we had cell phones?"

The woman had no idea that survival was at the top of their list.

"The storm's blowing over anyway. Telephone service might be back up at some point." Ellen patted Mara's hand. "I'm glad to see some new people. We've been alone here for the past three days. No other guests."

"Thought I saw someone hiking up here, but they never showed," George said.

Tanner skewered him with a look. "Really? When?"

"This morning. I trekked to the high point behind the lodge. There was a guy slogging along on cross-country skis way down at the bottom of the trail. Real diehard, right? To be out in these conditions? Maybe doing some hunting."

Hunting.

The Danish turned to stone in Mara's stomach.

"How about we go try and find ourselves some fresh clothes?" Tanner said.

Mara got to her feet. "Nice to meet you two."

Ellen looked disappointed that they were leaving. "Same. Maybe we'll see each other at dinner. Six o'clock. Pete promises something other than the hotdogs we've been eating for three days."

Mara nodded.

"Maybe we'll get another guest soon. It'll be a regular party. Here's hoping."

Tanner's hand tightened on Mara's shoulder. Exactly what they didn't want...another visitor. They found the small room near the front desk, lined with shelves crowded with bulging boxes. The lights didn't work but there was an electric lantern hanging on a hook which he turned on.

The boxes were open, the contents keeping them from closing.

Tanner sighed. "This might take a while."

She pulled a box free from the lower shelf and Tanner did the same.

"Do you think it was Eli or Vinny that George saw?"

"I assume so. Not the kind of conditions where anyone else would be out and about. After we get ourselves some clothes, I'll find the high point George was talking about and do some reconnaissance."

They pawed through the jumbled clothing, but many of the items were way too small for Tanner.

"Here," she said, holding out a yellow sweatshirt.

He grimaced. "That says, 'Top banana.'"

She started giggling.

"I don't think I can wear that."

"You don't think you'll look appealing?"

He laughed at the pun and it was good to hear. "Nice one, but no. Neon yellow is not in my color palette."

"How about this one?" She held a brown sweatshirt with white paw prints up. "It says, 'My dog is the boss of me.'"

"Better." He took the sweatshirt and they found him a pair of jeans only a smidge too short for his long legs.

Mara took down another box. "How do I look in pink?" The sweatshirt was covered in strawberry ice cream cones.

"You look gorgeous in anything."

She blushed and his face colored too.

"I meant, you know, I thought so when I saw you in your crime tech uniform and, uh, you look just as good now."

"In torn pants, a sweatshirt, and my hair done up in a rubber band? I think there may actually be pine needles glued to the back of my jacket."

He didn't look at her this time, lifting down another box. "I stand by my statement."

He thought she was gorgeous? Unsure what to do with her own discomfiture, she pulled out a pair of jeans that were way too baggy, but doable if she rolled up the hem and used the belt she'd found in another box. All of it was intact and warm and it could be zebra striped or neon polka-dotted for all she cared. She'd have dry clothes that appeared relatively clean. What a treat.

And Tanner said you're gorgeous.

She scolded herself for her foolish emotions and shoveled the extra clothes back into the box.

Britta whined.

They both stared at her.

"Is someone coming?"

Tanner shook his head. "She's alerted on something in here."

"In here? But how could…?" Her words trailed off as Tanner got down the boxes they'd unpacked one by one. The last one, the one she'd just put back on the shelf caused the dog to sit and stare at Tanner. A signal.

He dumped out the contents in front of Britta. The dog nosed through the pile, tossing up garments with her snout until she'd separated a glove from the batch. She thumped one paw on the floor.

Mara went cold as Tanner picked up the black glove. "Eli's?"

Tanner didn't answer.

"How could it be here? Pete said it's only us, and Ellen and George."

Pete poked his head in, and Mara jumped.

"Sorry for scaring you." He eyed the glove in Tanner's hand. "Is that yours? I found it at the bottom of the trail when I checked this morning. Figured someone must have gone hiking real early."

This morning… Her throat went dry.

"No, it's not mine," Tanner said. "Not Mara's either."

"Then it'll live in the lost and found, I guess. Anyway, I was gonna tell you all not to go off trail. Those cliffs behind us are real scenic, and people love to scope out the Flint Trail which extends from our property to the cliff face, but the snow looks unstable. Until the state transportation department clears it, we have to be on alert for avalanches."

Avalanches, Mara thought ruefully. Why not? They'd experienced every other type of hazard on the journey.

Tanner nodded at Pete. "Aside from the trail we came up on. Any other safe routes out of here?"

Pete quirked a brow at Tanner. "Not really. Like I just said, cliffs behind us are unstable and hard to navigate anyway. Even if you risked it heading out that way, it's still a twenty-mile trek to any kind of civilization. It's why people come here…the remoteness. We're in for a patch of good weather. Snow will settle nicely along the trail back down if you really want to scram today."

Tanner didn't answer.

After a moment, Pete gestured to the boxes of items. "Take whatever you want. Getting way too cluttered in here."

Cluttered. Crowded. Smothered. She stared at the

black glove in Tanner's hand. Eli and Vinny were coming. She couldn't leave the tiny room fast enough.

Tanner hustled them upstairs. The late afternoon shadows were sliding into evening darkness made gloomier by the weak power supply. At least the upstairs still had power.

Eli had been close enough to drop that glove. It was a matter of time now before one or both of the killers arrived on scene. Should they bolt? But with only one safe route to and from the lodge, they'd be easy pickings for Eli who might be counting on them to do that very thing. Maybe the glove drop hadn't been an accident. It was designed to flush them out right into an ambush. He had to send a message.

George was leaving his room as they passed. "Howdy."

"Any chance you got a signal?" Tanner asked.

"Believe it or not, yes, but only for a few moments."

Tanner's heart leaped. A few moments was all he required. He tried to keep the intensity out of his next question. "Oh, yeah? Where?"

"The attic." He pointed to a narrow staircase at the end of the hallway.

"Appreciate it." Tanner forced a smile as George disappeared down the squeaky corridor. Unlocking the door to Mara's room, he and Britta rechecked every corner, and each creak of the wooden floorboards cranked his nerves tighter.

"I'll be back. Britta, watch." He was going to trot out the door when Mara's expression stopped him. She looked stricken. Why?

"I'm sorry," she blurted.

"Sorry for what?"

"Starting this whole thing in motion. No matter what we do we can't shake Eli. If I'd trusted the team…"

He stopped, took her hands and tried to ease away her sudden recrimination. "You had good reasons for doing what you did. Eli and his guy are the villains here and you know what?"

When she didn't answer, he tipped her chin to meet his eyes. Tiny crystal tears turned her irises iridescent. "We are going to get back home."

"I was so sure for so long, but now…"

"Now I'm sure for both of us. We're going back home," he repeated.

She bit her lip.

As if it was the most natural thing in the world, he kissed her. Could he share his conviction, ease her fear and his own by a simple touch of their lips? Her mouth soft and warm, fitting perfectly against his own. A delicious warmth trickled through his body, zooming straight to his heart. He'd meant to be the encourager, but he found he wanted to stay lost in her warmth, her courage.

He heard her sigh, a gentle murmur like a summer breeze. Everything in him wanted to be close to her for longer than the space of one kiss. That would mean letting go of himself, of his duty, freeing himself from the solemn pact he'd signed the day Allie passed away and took his heart with her. *No, Tanner. No.* He broke away from the kiss.

"I…uh, I don't want you to worry. None of this is your fault."

She looked shocked, speechless.

"I'll be back," he said hurriedly. "Lock the door and don't open it for anyone but me."

Mara's eyes were still wide, but she nodded, one hand going to Britta who'd taken up position at her side.

The whole situation was confusing him, weakening his convictions and beliefs. *God, what am I meant to be doing here?*

His brain answered quickly before his heart could weigh in. *Saving Mara and getting her home.*

Lips tingling, he purposely pushed away his reckless decision to kiss her. He climbed the precariously steep stairwell which ended in the attic, a large dusty space with a peaked roof and narrowed walls. The haphazard arrangement of mismatched furniture hinted that it had been used at one time for a meeting room. A telescope was aimed out the lift-up window.

In the middle of the room he tried his phone. No signal. He moved to another corner with no better result. The stairs creaked behind him. He whirled, reflexively reaching for the weapon holstered under his untucked shirt.

"Hi, Pete." He hoped the innkeeper hadn't noticed his reaction.

"Hey. Whatcha doing up here?"

The truth was always the most convincing. "George said he got a signal. Figured I'd give it a try."

"Happens sometimes. You're real eager to get a call out, huh? Vacation emergency?"

"You know how it goes," Tanner said vaguely.

"I know how it goes for most folks who come here. They're happy to be away from their troubles. They sort of sink into the quiet of the place and it sinks into them too."

Tanner's stomach tightened.

"Not you, though." Pete stroked his flyaway beard. "You're real anxious."

Tanner remained silent as Pete's gaze lasered into him.

"Know what I think, Tanner?"

He widened his stance a fraction. "What's that, Pete?"

"I think you've got a weapon there on your belt."

He froze, hands dangling unencumbered. They looked at each other across the dusty attic. "Let's say I do, hypothetically, Pete. Would that be a problem for you? If it was legally owned and registered and all that, I mean?"

Pete's eyes narrowed. "You mean, like hypothetically if it were a work tool? Like maybe, you were a cop or something?"

Tanner kept his tone flat, expressionless. "Like I said, would that be a problem for you, Pete?"

"If you were here pretending to be some Joe Shmoe and his cousin?"

Tanner stayed silent.

Pete shook his head. "I pegged you as law enforcement the moment you walked in. You can tell a cop, if you know what you're looking for. They got this wary streak, no matter where they happen to be, in or out of uniform. This invisible wall they keep people behind until they know which side of the enemy line they fall on."

"What's your point?"

Pete lifted a shoulder. "No point. If you were a cop, that'd explain a lot of things, is all." He folded his arms across his chest. "And if you were in the mood to chat… I'd tell you that my brother Donnie was a cop in Chicago for twenty years before he died. I loved my brother and I miss him so bad it hurts some days. I'd also tell you that I got a great respect for cops, especially those who put themselves out for people in need. Donnie was that kind of guy. A good cop, a good man."

The words sounded supportive, Pete's demeanor sincere, but Tanner still wasn't certain on which side of the enemy line Pete stood. Some people were very accomplished liars. He stayed quiet.

"Anyway, just wanted to get that off my chest and tell you that if you need anything, I'm your man and I'll do what I can to help you and your…cousin." He pointed to the window. "There's a tiny balcony out there, only big enough for one, basically. Gives me the willies to be on it, but sometimes you can snag a signal. Dunno why but something about the angle to the satellite I guess. One of those mysteries of life. No guarantees. Thought it might help to know that." He turned and left.

Friend or foe? One way to find out. Pete's claim needed testing, pronto.

He turned the lever and pushed the double windows open, cold air barreling at him like a freight train. As Pete promised, outside was a miniscule balcony, maybe four foot square, piled six inches high with snow. He eased out, hoping the structure was rated for a six-foot guy. The metal creaked ominously under his feet as he shuffled into the snow. The view was incomparable, the frozen cliffs behind the inn covered by their deadly blanket, the slopes around dotted by thick forests of

pines that scented the crystal-clean air. He fished out
his phone and sent a text, praying it would go through.

Asher. Trapped. He included the location. Vinny and
Eli closing in. Copy?

The little dots swirled and swirled. He twisted on the
balcony, leaning out into space, pain radiating through
his ribs. *One message, that's all I need. Come on.*

No amount of squirming was changing the outcome.
His message would not send, no matter how he con-
torted. He felt like hurling the phone into the snow. The
current millennium was chock-full of cutting-edge tech-
nology and he couldn't so much as send one lousy text.

As he muttered at his phone, the dots swirled and
stopped. In his surprise he almost dropped the cell as
the reply appeared.

Copy that. Mobilizing now.

A reply. He'd actually gotten a reply. His chest prac-
tically exploded with joy. He clutched the phone, staring at the next message materializing on the screen.

Possibly twenty-four hours ETA. Injuries?

Jubilantly, he typed the response. Minor only. Holding
in position until your arrival.

Copy that. Another set of swirling dots. Extremely
relieved to hear from you. Tell Mara…

And then his screen went blank. No matter how he
wriggled or repositioned, leaning precariously over the
balcony railing, he could not restore the signal. He stood
there, breathing hard.

Finally. Communication with the outside world. The team knew, and they were on the way. Energy flooded through him, hope resurging. He couldn't wait to tell Mara.

God had given him the minute he needed.

And God willing, He'd give them the strength to hold on until the team arrived.

ELEVEN

Mara's heart rattled as Tanner related what had happened.

"I still don't know if Pete's trustworthy, but thanks to his tip, help is on the way."

Rescue. At long last. She clutched her arms around herself to hold her emotions in check. The delight in his eyes sparked through her soul. "I can hardly believe it. We're actually going to get out of here?"

He grinned the widest smile she'd seen from him in all the time she'd known him. "It's a matter of hours before the team arrives. By this time tomorrow they'll be on scene and hopefully Eli and Vinny will be in custody."

She tried to make the incredible thought sink in. Her brother and the officers would arrive. And then it would all be over. "We're going home."

"We are. No more running, Mara. No more hiding. No more eating stale Danishes and borrowing clothes and looking over our shoulders every moment."

She whooped. Britta barked. Tanner scooped her up in an embrace and lifted her off the ground, kissing her cheek. She threw her arms around his neck as he twirled her in a circle. Slowly she tipped her head up and he kissed her on the lips, warm and gentle and perfect as if his mouth had been made just to kiss hers. Her heart thumped giddily when the kiss was over.

He put her down, but kept his arms circled around the small of her back. "You've been an absolute tiger to endure all of this."

"We endured it together. I wouldn't have survived if you and Britta hadn't shown up at that cabin when you did." It seemed like ages ago that Tanner had extricated her from the shack as Vinny and Eli were about to break in. Surreal was the best way to describe it. They'd been struggling shoulder to shoulder, heart to heart ever since.

The moment stretched between them, lovely and fragile, her arms encircling his neck and his palms on the small of her back. Their eyes met and there was such a world of possibility in his coffee-colored gaze, an intelligence that drew her, his compassion captivating. Would he kiss her again? It seemed a possibility as he lingered there, gaze roving her face.

"Back to the real world," he murmured, giving her one more squeeze before he let her go.

Pain cleaved deep in her chest. The real world…so what was happening in her heart here and now wasn't the same reality he was experiencing.

Wise up, Mara. Soon she'd be returned to her little apartment and Tanner and Britta to theirs. They'd see each other at work, at the coffee machine, at trainings, maybe. Regular life, mundane moments. Her ebullience was pricked, deflated. Why couldn't he feel what she had? That their lives were unalterably changed now?

Interwoven in a way they hadn't been before? But that only worked if both people wanted the connection. She summoned a smile. "We're going to have some stories to tell the team, aren't we?"

He laughed. "That's for sure."

"It'll be so strange…being back." She thought about how brave she'd become while on the run, how silly it now felt not to share her thoughts. "I… I'll miss seeing you every day." She looked up at him, his haggard face, the lines of fatigue that grooved around his mouth…and in his eyes she saw the door shutting out the flash of light.

It felt as if the door had slammed on her too, bruising and breaking her. But it didn't need to, did it? Maybe if she had the courage to speak the feelings into existence… Should she say it? The truth that was bumbling around in her heart? Risk embarrassment and awkwardness? Potentially endure all that to clearly express her desire for a relationship with him?

Before she'd have closed her mouth, shut away her thoughts, put her head down and pretended not to see or feel what was knocking inside. But the Mara she'd been before did not exist anymore. God had changed her, challenged her and coaxed her to step out of the shadows.

So she tipped her face to his and spoke. "I have to be honest, Tanner. You're an amazing man. I've always thought so, but running through the wilderness avoiding a killer has proved me right." She tried to smile. He didn't return it. "I'd hoped…" She took a breath, shrinking inside. "I hoped we could continue a relationship when we get back home. I want to keep you in my life, as more than just a colleague." There. She'd said it and immediately knew it was a mistake.

The closing door hadn't been her imagination. Nor was his slight step backward, his hands burrowing deep into his pockets. Pain welled up inside her. She wanted to be with Tanner. He didn't feel the same. That much was obvious. What had she done revealing her feelings so boldly?

Awkwardness and embarrassment were now the reality between them. The words couldn't be unspoken. He didn't want her, not in the way she wanted him and he was embarrassed that she'd forced him to reveal it. Maybe it was damage from Allie's death, or maybe she simply wasn't the woman Tanner Ford was willing to risk his heart for, like she hadn't been for Jonas. She wasn't sure which.

"I'm sorry…" He said, hand raised as if to touch her cheek. "You're one of a kind, Mara, truly, but I'm not looking for a relationship."

"Because of what you lost, or because of me?" She hadn't meant to sound abrupt, but he must have taken it that way because he sighed.

The moment stretched out before he replied. "I don't want to experience what I did with Allie. It made me forget who I am. I became some sort of robot, plowing through days, believing it wasn't ever going to get better. It did, slowly and agonizingly. Two years later, I can live with the loss, even feel happiness now and enjoy things that come my way, but not relationships, not deep ones, the kind with profound connection like I had with her. Nothing is worth risking that pain again."

Nothing, and no one. She should stop right there.

Tanner had made his wishes clear. But there was so much anguish and fear bubbling below the surface of his explanation, she felt convicted to speak. "I read this quote once from C.S. Lewis. He said the only way to protect yourself from hurt is to lock your heart away where it can't be reached. My dad kind of did that, I think. He was so ashamed at what he'd done cheating on Asher's mother that he detached for years. Kept his feelings locked away and didn't really allow Mom and me to love him too deeply." She paused a beat. "He regretted it before he got sick."

His expression darkened. "Different," he said. "I lost the love of my life. I didn't betray her."

"No, you didn't." She felt the sorrow that underpinned his whole existence. "Tanner, I never met Allie but I'm pretty sure she wouldn't have wanted you to die too."

He blinked in surprise. "I didn't. I'm still in the world, in case you haven't noticed."

"In it, but a little removed. I've lived like that too."

His brows furrowed. "You don't understand, Mara. God let me heal and I'm grateful for that. He didn't mend me so I could get ripped apart again. What would be the sense of that?"

"He healed you so you could keep on living and loving while you're at it. I get that it's not me, but I hope you'll allow the possibility of a future with someone down the road. You have so much to offer, it would be a shame if you didn't." She was aghast at her forthrightness.

He started to speak, then stopped and shook his head. "I can't speak for someday. I'm sorry I can't be what you want, Mara. You really do deserve the best."

It dawned on her that her own ego was tripping her up. She had the answer now. It wasn't that Tanner couldn't love again, but he didn't love *her*. The thought lashed her like the flick of a whip. Tanner was a kind man and the "I don't want to love anyone" would hurt less than "I just don't love *you*." How humiliating. What was she doing talking to him this way? Her cheeks turned to flame. "It's okay. You don't have to say any more."

"It's not…"

"Tanner, we've been through a lot. Please don't say 'it's not you—it's me.' At least spare me that."

He closed his mouth, since that was likely exactly what he'd been about to say.

The fire in her cheeks spread to her stomach, churning flames that burned her from the inside out. "I put you in an awkward position. It was uncalled for. I apologize."

"My fault. I… The kiss… I got caught up in the moment and I sent mixed signals."

She could not allow the mortification to continue. "We've been through a mess and we both got caught up at one point or another. I will be grateful until the end of my days that you and Britta saved me." She rustled up another smile and stuck out her palm. "Friends for life I hope?"

He shook, pain twitching his mouth. "Friends for life."

"Great." She searched desperately for a way to get out of the conversation with a shred of dignity. She clutched at her watch. "It will be a while before Asher arrives. I think I'll take one last bath and maybe a nap for old time's sake. I'll be safe here with Britta. You probably want to pack or something."

She didn't wait for an answer, turning away from him. The adjoining door squeaked as he pulled it almost closed.

"Mara, what in the world were you thinking?" she whispered to herself, body still alight with mortification. *You basically confessed your love to a man who doesn't love you back.*

Britta cocked an ear and bonked Mara with her nose. Mara sank to the floor and caressed her under the chin. "It's all right, girl. Just admitting my own silliness aloud. You won't tell, will you?" Britta licked her.

The warmth in her cheeks would dissipate, but the gap that opened up inside her at that moment would remain unfilled. Maybe there would be another man in her life someday, but he wouldn't be Tanner Ford.

He told you. He made it clear. Your mistake, not his.

Before the tears had a chance to kick in, she hurried into the bathroom. The hot water did not relax her enough for a nap, though she forced herself to lie on the bed, desperately trying to keep her mind off what had transpired with Tanner. He tapped on her door when it was time for dinner and they went downstairs. Ellen and George were there, Ellen eager to chat.

"Finally finished all the Danish," she said. "There's a whole new menu at our disposal, cheese sandwiches and corn chips."

Mara felt like she'd rather be anywhere but in that dining room trying to make conversation.

Tanner settled on eating a sandwich from the platter Pete had provided along with a bag of chips and a soda.

She forced herself to eat hers too, listening to Ellen chatter away. "Tail end of the storm. The snow accumulation is huge, but sooner or later the plow will clear the main road, so we've decided to get while the getting's good."

Mara looked up in surprise. "You're leaving?"

George yawned. "Uh-huh. Right after we eat."

"Really? You don't want to wait until morning?" Mara said. For some reason the thought of being alone in the inn with only Tanner and Pete depressed her.

Ellen nodded. "Weather looks clear enough for us to make the trek back down and we've had a lot of practice snowshoeing. As long as we keep away from the cliffs where the snow's unstable, we should be okay. We've got a snowmobile parked at the bottom that should get us back to the cabin we're heading to in less than three hours." She brushed her fingertips on a napkin. "Are you two staying much longer?"

Tanner crunched a chip. "Just until some friends of ours arrive."

Ellen nodded. "Enjoy your visit and safe travels to you all."

They said goodbye. In a few minutes, Ellen and George had fetched their gear and departed.

"And then there were three," she said.

Tanner finished his sandwich. "Four if you count Britta."

"And I do. She's my canine hero." Mara kissed Britta on the nose. It was easier to be close to the boxer than Tanner. After what she'd said… She cringed inwardly. Fortunately, dogs never held a person accountable for the drivel that spilled from their mouths.

Determinedly, she forced down the remainder of the sandwich, though her hunger had all but evaporated. In a matter of hours they'd be okay, headed back to Olympia. She could forget what had happened between them. He'd be the genial coworker and she'd be the friendly crime scene tech and they'd never bring up the humiliating conversation again.

Tanner was busily scanning the rafters, the stone fireplace with crackling logs. He'd bent Pete's ear about the generator and solar panels, the water and septic systems. Pete trotted off to go get the blueprints to show him.

Best to get the conversation going again on a neutral topic. "Is this the kind of place you envision owning someday, off the grid?"

He didn't look at her but his smile was warm and dreamy. "Yes, but I pictured Alaska, not Washington. The idea's been calling my name louder lately, to be honest. Plenty of work there in law enforcement. Maybe I won't wait for another ten years before I look for a property. Not after what we survived here. God might be trying to tell me to get my rear in gear."

In another state, with another department.

A pang of grief cut through her. "That'd be nice," she mumbled. "Off-the-grid and all the peace and quiet a person could want."

He nodded. "Long as there's heat and running water, right?"

"Right. I think I'll go upstairs and read for a while." She plucked a battered paperback from the bookshelf. She read the title aloud. "*Countdown to Rescue.* Appropriate."

He discarded his empty can into the recycle bin. "We'll see you to your room, then I'll take Britta out for a potty break."

Mara took the stairs quickly, not wanting to allow time for any more chitchat. She'd used up her supply. Tanner and Britta checked the room and they left. Locked in, she collapsed onto the mattress. What a night. The best she could hope for was Asher's quick arrival and a speedy end to the whole ordeal. Her zinging nerves would not allow her to relax, so after a few minutes she peeked out the window. Asher and Britta were easing along the front path that Pete had spent the morning laboriously shoveling clear. It was hemmed in on both sides by walls of white. In twenty feet they took a turn and were swallowed from view.

She pressed a palm to the window, the glass cold against her skin.

Lie down, Mara. Let them go.

She'd listen for the sound of their return. Tanner would knock and she'd cheerfully tell him she was fine. He'd insist Britta act as her canine babysitter and she'd agree. Then it would be a matter of trying to sleep until the next day when her life would change again. Thrilling and sad at the same time.

Stripping off her socks and shoes, she pressed her toes to the hardwood and did a Pilates stretch. Muscles unkinked, she tried to breathe away the embarrassment and regret, to relax herself for what was to come. As she straightened, arms lifted overhead, she heard the sound of a key in the door lock.

Why would Tanner come through that way instead of the adjoining door?

Who else would have a key to the room? Pete, obviously. But Tanner hadn't trusted him. He had no reason to let himself in her room. The knob turned.

She was already sprinting for the bathroom when the door was flung wide.

Vinny lunged in. He barreled straight at her, knocking her to the floor. She hit hard, the breath driven out of her. He planted his knee in the small of her back and reached to grip her hair.

She squirmed free, slammed herself at the chest of drawers, reaching for anything she could use to defend herself. There was a ceramic lamp, but in her terror she knocked it to the floor. "Leave me alone," she screamed. Maybe Pete would hear. Come to her rescue.

"Quiet," Vinny snarled. He grabbed the waistband of her jeans and tossed her down. She rolled onto her back and crab walked toward the dresser. Vinny had the beginnings of a beard, his breath hot and sour in the small space. The hairs bristled on the back of her neck. Over her terror she saw him click open a knife.

"I'm done freezing my bones in this wasteland," he said, punctuating each word with a point of his knife. "Been tracking you through the middle of nowhere for months. Should have dumped this job and Eli when you escaped us at the cabin and let him kill you himself. At least I'll get my paycheck finally."

"No, you won't."

He laughed, showing tar-stained teeth. "Cop and his dog are too far away to hear you. This isn't going to take long."

Her fingers found the fallen lamp. As he drove the knife downward, she thrust it out. The blade skittered against the ceramic, carving off chips that fluttered to the floor.

"Help," she screamed.

"No one's coming, Mara." He swiped his knife out again, ripping through the lampshade.

Her panic left her shaking so hard she almost lost her grip. With a curse, he wrestled the knife free and raised his arm to strike again. She swung the lamp at him. The blocky object connected with his chin, momentarily knocking him back, giving her a precious window to escape. She leaped past him to the door but he grabbed her ankle and she went down hard, her kneecaps cracking into the wood. Tanner and Britta were too far away to hear, but where was Pete? She screamed again and again at her loudest volume.

He clawed to get a grip on her shirt, to immobilize her so he could plunge the knife into her chest. She snatched the backpack from the floor next to the bed and swung it around with all her strength. It was an awkward motion, but the thermos inside whammed against his temple. The impact knocked him sideways and sent the knife skittering loose. While he lunged for it, she wrenched open the door and tumbled out, stumbling, hands outstretched, impacting the far wall.

"Help," she screamed again.

Where was Pete?

She half fell, half ran down the stairs, screaming as loudly as she could over her panting breaths. Vinny was only a few steps behind her, swearing and staggering as he too took the stairs. She remembered the baseball bat that Pete kept behind the reception desk.

She hit the ground floor, turned the corner and dove

behind the desk, rattling a tray of clean mugs balanced there. She'd have only one moment to defend herself. She grabbed for the bat just as Vinny's hand closed around her sweatshirt, yanking her away from her only means of protection.

Britta was trotting back to the inn, Tanner right behind when she stiffened and whined. Her nose went from side to side as she picked up a scent. A scent? She wasn't behaving the way she would if she was tracking Eli. More like she'd heard a disturbing sound.

He stopped for only a moment to text. Mara. Trouble. She likely wouldn't receive it, but he had to try. Mouth dry, he took off at a sprint. Britta raced beside him over the snowy ground, beelining for the inn.

Had he missed something? Mara was locked safely in her room, surely?

His stomach dropped. Vinny or Eli could have been watching to see when Tanner would leave to let Britta out. Or maybe Pete wasn't the good guy he portrayed and he'd alerted the two the moment Tanner had left? He was breathing hard now, and so was Britta, churning up bits of snow, skidding on slick patches. They were only yards away from the front door.

Had he blown it? Was he going to be too late?

Britta raced to the inn's front door. She knew someone had arrived who didn't belong. Someone intent on harming Mara. He commanded Britta to get behind him as he pulled his weapon and burst inside.

TWELVE

Tanner skidded to a stop in the lobby. Vinny was behind the reception desk, fist bunched in the fabric of Mara's jacket. The knife he held in his other hand was poised to plunge between her shoulder blades.

"Stop right there," Tanner thundered, sighting down his weapon. "Drop the knife, Vinny."

Dark eyes glittering, Vinny swung Mara in front of him like a shield, sliding the blade around to her throat. "Put it down, or I cut her."

Mara's mouth was a tight line of terror, fingers digging into his forearm as she struggled to keep him from choking her. A mug from a tray on the table wobbled and fell with a crash.

"Bad idea to hurt her, Vinny. You're not getting out of here, so at least make it easy on yourself. Let Eli take the fall." Tanner's body was tingling with adrenaline. He had no shot, not without risking Mara. Britta barked from behind him, but she maintained her position.

Vinny shook his head. "Nothing about this stupid job has been easy. I'm not leaving until I do what I'm gettin' paid for. In too deep now to bug out."

"No you're not. You can stop this."

"And what? You'll let me go? Uh-huh. Sure."

Tanner tried to edge to the side, but Vinny held Mara close. He could see no way out that didn't involve injury to her.

Mara stared at Tanner and blinked twice at him. What was she trying to say? His palms felt slippery around the weapon. Whatever she was planning could get her killed. *No, don't try anything.* He willed her to understand.

Five seconds later Mara reared backward, driving her head into Vinny's chin. He let out a grunt. When he recoiled, Mara somersaulted over the check-in desk and into the lobby, stumbling and falling on the floor near Tanner's feet.

"Britta," Tanner yelled.

Britta ran to Mara, tugged at her sleeve, urging her up, and yanked her out of Vinny's range.

Vinny's mouth streamed with blood from a split lip. With a howl of outrage, he hurled the tray full of coffee mugs.

Tanner held up a forearm to block the missiles as they rained down, smashing on impact. Vinny used the distraction to bolt. With Tanner and his revolver standing between him and the door, Vinny spun on his heel and took the stairs two at a time, the knife still clutched in his fist. Mara and Britta were crouched in the corner, safe for the moment. He charged toward the stairs.

"Tanner," Mara screamed, but he hit the stairs after Vinny, trying to predict the guy's next move. There weren't many avenues of escape on the second story. He could wrench open a window, jump out maybe. Or lie in wait for an opportunity to kill Tanner so he could get to

Mara. That wasn't going to happen. With his head start, Vinny reached the top with Tanner ten steps behind him. Pete appeared on the landing.

"Look out," Tanner yelled.

Pete reacted. With one sweeping motion, he pulled a framed print off the wall and brought it down squarely on Vinny's head. In a river of broken glass, Vinny's body snapped back and cartwheeled. Tanner had only a moment to flatten himself against the railing to avoid being taken down by the flailing limbs.

Vinny tumbled along the remaining steps, landing in an untidy heap on the ground floor. Tanner plunged after him. Britta barked with urgency. She looked as though she wanted to run to Tanner.

"Stay, Britta," he yelled as he sprinted back down the steps. Britta knew enough in an emergency to keep close to whomever Tanner directed, no matter how upset she was. And he wanted Britta and Mara to stay well clear of the fallen Vinny until he was dead certain Vinny was immobilized.

Vinny was lying on his back, arms flung wide, the knife loose in his grip.

Tanner was on him in a moment, stripping the knife away and sliding it out of reach, checking him for other weapons. Vinny's eyes were closed. "Hey," he said, tapping Vinny on the shoulder.

Pete stared. "Is he dead?"

Vinny was stone still, a goose egg bump rising on his forehead. His chest rose and fell. Tanner got a strong pulse from his wrist.

"Alive. Get the handcuffs and zipties from the backpack in my room, okay Pete?"

Pete disappeared to complete the errand.

"Mara…" he called over his pounding heart. He risked a quick look at her.

"I'm okay," she whispered, clinging to Britta's collar. "Are you sure he's alive?"

He knelt and checked the pulse at Vinny's throat again. "Breathing and he has a pulse."

He heard Mara gulp.

Pete came down the stairs, holding on to the railing. Tanner noticed he had a violet bruise on his cheekbone.

"What happened?"

"He got me when I was cleaning Ellen and George's room. Knocked me out with one punch and took the keys." Pete glared at the fallen man. "Glad I had a chance to return the favor."

Tanner wiped his sweaty brow. "Much appreciated."

Pete shrugged. "Told you I was a fan of cops."

Tanner smiled. "And I'm now a loyal fan of innkeepers."

Mara stood and started to move closer but he stopped her. "I'm going to cuff him before anybody moves." Since the man was obviously injured, he secured his hands in front instead of behind. "He needs a doctor."

Pete shook his head. "Don't think there's a way to get him to one, just yet. I'll try to get a signal again in the attic, but what do we do in the meantime?"

"I'll carry him to Ellen and George's room and secure him to the bed. At least there's heat and electricity up there."

Pete shrugged. "Okay. I guess. I worked as an EMT for a while, so I can monitor his vitals. Ironic, since I gather he was itchin' to kill both of you. If there was any justice, he'd be dead."

"God's got His own reasons why people live or die." The words seemed to come out on their own. Once Tanner said it, the statement seemed to circle and echo in his own ears. God chose. He had decided not to allow Allie to be cured and Tanner had never wanted to experience that emotional punishment again, yet in the last few moments He'd also allowed Tanner and Pete to prevent Vinny from ending Mara's life. Why? It was dizzying trying to understand. And if he couldn't understand, how could he ever be certain he wouldn't feel excruciating loss again?

He couldn't. No guarantees, for him or anyone else. He found his pulse hammering double time when he allowed himself to consider what would have happened if he'd arrived a minute later. In a span of sixty seconds he might have lost Mara. Emotions he'd have to process when they were back in Olympia. He forced his body and brain into action.

Vinny was heavy and it required both Pete and Tanner to carry him up the stairs. They tried to jostle him as little as possible to prevent further injury. He released the cuffs and repositioned them, fastening one of Vinny's wrists to the bedpost without straining him too much and circling his ankles loosely with zip ties. He removed anything close to Vinny that he might use as a weapon if he roused, the lamp, the heavy alarm clock. He was as comfortable as the circumstances would allow, still nonresponsive but breathing steadily. Pete promised to check vitals after he tried for a signal.

Tanner wiped his brow and returned to the ground floor. He found Mara holding a paper towel to her arm.

Blood stained the white a brilliant red. His breath hitched as he ran to her. How hadn't he noticed she was hurt? Why hadn't she told him? "How bad?"

"Not bad."

He propelled her into a chair. "Sit. You could be going into shock."

"I'm not…"

But he hardly heard. He was spinning in circles. "Pete," he roared. "Where's a first aid kit?" But Pete was in the attic, too far away to hear. "I'll find it. It's probably behind the desk."

"I don't need a first aid kit."

Fumbling through the cabinets, he snatched up a clean towel and dropped to a knee in front of her. Britta whined, tail spinning in agitated circles as she shoved her head between them until he ordered her to sit.

He reached for the paper towel. "Let me see. Do you need stitches? Pete's got medical experience. Did you hit your head? You're trembling. Don't get up, you might fall."

She stood anyway, setting him back on his heels. "Tanner."

Her tone was sharp, popping through his mental fuzz. "What?"

"I got a nick from one of the broken mugs. That's why I'm bleeding. It's a teeny cut, nothing more."

"Oh. Okay, but you…"

"I'm trembling," she said, chin quivering, "because… well a woman's allowed to tremble if she's nearly been killed by a man who's been tracking her for months, right?" He heard a sob building underneath.

"Yes." He got up, reaching for her.

"And I've been strong, through all this, haven't I? Strong, through months of being hunted and stalked and freezing and starving."

"Absolutely."

A tear trickled down her cheek and he reached to brush it away. "Real strong, Mara. A tiger, like I said."

She cried freely now, as he gathered her to him, the tears hot over his hands as he cupped her cheeks.

"Pete's been hurt," she choked out, "but it's still not over. Vinny's caught but Eli's not and the team isn't here yet, so this horrible dangerous limbo continues. And if you hadn't come in, Vinny would have…" Her emotion strangled the words.

"But I did." He folded her into his chest, rubbing her back and holding her tight. "And you're the strongest, most amazing woman I've ever met. That head butt and somersault over the counter were phenomenal."

"They were?" Her voice was a high squeak.

"Yes, they were, honey. A perfect ten. And you know what else?"

"What?"

"It's okay to cry."

"Good," she said, the tears running in earnest.

He held her until the sobs subsided into quiet sniffs. By then, Pete had returned. "No signal, but Vinny's vitals are steady." He fetched a first aid kit and bandaged the nick on Mara's forearm.

She didn't want to go rest in her room and Tanner didn't blame her, not with Vinny occupying the space directly adjacent. If only the downstairs was warm, he'd insist she stay there. He itched to hike to a high spot outside, try and summon Asher and fill him in, but he would not leave Mara's side, not until Eli was in custody.

Mara was right. It wasn't over. There was time yet for Eli to make a last stand.

And Tanner and Britta would be sure he didn't get the chance.

As the sun began to sink behind the pines, Mara tried to rest. Britta was with Tanner, patrolling the exterior of the building, checking doors, windows for any sign of Eli. They'd have worked their way to the far side of the inn by now. Pete was watching Vinny who had not shown any signs of consciousness.

All her emotions were jumbled into a tangled ball. She still burned with the embarrassment of her admission and arrogance. Telling Tanner she wanted a relationship with him, refusing to acknowledge that he didn't want one in exchange. Now she had the trauma of needing him for comfort after she'd almost been executed. Well, wouldn't anyone need some support at that kind of moment? She paced the tiny room, shoving the remains of the broken lamp into the trash can.

Terror and mortification were a horrible combination that made her stomach churn. She flopped onto the bed, pulling the pillow over her face with a groan. Between the two situations, she felt like she was unraveling. At the present, she wanted to dig a hole and bury herself in the snow so deep even Britta couldn't find her.

A beep, followed by a crackle of static made her sit up. Had she fallen asleep and dreamed the noise? She heard it again, a soft buzzing.

A radio?

She dove to her knees and looked under the bed where she found a black handheld radio unit. Vinny must have dropped it during their tussle. Another crackle and a whisper sent terror coursing along her nerves.

"Where are you?" the voice snarled.

Her body recoiled. Eli. Of course. He was trying to contact his fallen cohort, Vinny.

She thought about going for Tanner, but fury unlike anything she'd ever known swept through her. The months of misery, physical and mental, the feel of Vinny's knife against her throat…it all hardened into a shard of rage that threatened to flay her apart. She squeezed the radio button.

"Vinny is unconscious and handcuffed," she spat. "And you're going to be arrested, Eli. For your gun running, and what you did to Jonas and Stacey…" The words nearly choked her. "And what you did to me. It's over. You lose. How does it feel?"

There was a long silent pause as she gripped the radio, hot blood cascading through her veins. She tried to get hold of her emotions and allow reason to return. What was she doing here, compromising a piece of evidence? Talking with a murderer? Had she totally lost it in her months as a fugitive? She was about to put the radio down and run for Tanner when it crackled again.

"You've been a pain in my behind since the moment I met you, Mara. So aloof and self-righteous. You thought you were some kind of hotshot, didn't you? Had to stick your nose in my business when you could have just done your job and fawned all over your big brother."

She was shaking with rage. "Oh, I did my job. You were using those lodges for illegal purposes, and I knew it. I set out to bring you down once I saw you loaded those boxes into Stacey's lodge. All I needed was a few good photos to take to the team. I'm only sorry I didn't get the chance, but the team followed the trail when I left off and what do you know? We caught a rat. Busted, Eli. Got you for the smuggling. Now we'll get you for the murders too." Glee flooded her senses. *They'd won. He'd lost.*

"Not gonna happen, Mara. I can convince a jury, no matter what the evidence says. I'm extremely charismatic." The words were filled with venom. "All you did was cost me time."

His bravado didn't completely cover the tiny shred of uncertainty. She'd gotten to him now, and she relished the feeling of being in control. "Enjoy your self-delusion while you can. It doesn't matter if you kill me or not. Regardless, the team will make sure you go to jail or spend the rest of your life living as a fugitive, the way you forced me to live. That's even better justice than I could have hoped for." She laughed. "You've wasted your precious freedom chasing me and it's gotten you nothing."

He was breathing heavily. "But I'm not done yet, Mara."

"Yes, you are." It was past time to get Tanner. "Gotta go, Eli, but I'll give your regards to Vinny. Maybe he can be a cell mate for you." She was about to drop the radio.

"All right. Tell you what. Maybe I'll walk right over to that inn and surrender myself to your cop right now, but you need to do one thing first."

"What's that?"

"Look out your window."

Something in his smug tone jangled alarm bells in her stomach. She inched to the curtain, careful to stay out of view in case he was ready to take a shot. At first she saw nothing in the failing sunlight. Then a gleam of yellow caught her attention, thrown from behind the snow-clad bushes.

She could not identify it. In her backpack was a banged-up pair of binoculars which she fetched and angled out the window, still staying out of full view. A beam of the setting sun roved over the object. The binoculars brought it into focus.

A sweater, yellow and worn. The same one from the keychain photo she'd kept all these months.

Her blood turned to ice.

She could not see the patch on the left elbow but she knew it was there because she'd sewn it herself. It was her father's favorite sweater, one he never seemed to shed since he was always cold.

Through the cascade of panic, she rallied a threat of logic. Eli was bluffing. The sweater wasn't proof that Eli had her father, only that he possessed the garment. A simple trick to terrorize her. Her dad was in a safe house. Asher arranged it.

But what if he *had* gotten to her father somehow? Paid a worker at the facility for information, or to follow Asher when he'd relocated their father. That could be why Eli had been absent the past few days, leaving Vinny to terrorize her. He could have returned to Olympia and snatched her father from the safe house. Her muscles pulsed with terror. Her frail father, confused and vulnerable…

She hoped her voice wouldn't shake when she spoke into the radio. "You don't have him."

"So arrogant, Mara. When will you learn not to underestimate me? I've collected a whole network of spies. It wasn't hard. Got him stowed away someplace safe and only I know where. I had to listen to Daddy dear ramble on and on about his 'Marbles' before I locked him up. He thinks you're some kind of perfect child. If he only knew."

Her stomach knotted. Her nickname. The one only her father used. How would Eli know that unless…? But he could have heard Dad rambling to the caregivers? Paid one for information.

Eli laughed. "Poor Daddy's probably getting hungry since he's all alone where I imprisoned him. There's only so long an old guy like that can survive, especially without his blood pressure pills and his glaucoma drops and that stuff he takes for acid reflux."

He knew her father's medications. He knew everything.

He paused. "So silent, Mara. Not so cocky anymore, are we? Yeah. I told Daddy I'd let him out if you cooperate, but if you're not in the mood…"

With trembling fingers she pressed the radio button to respond. "You don't have him. You could have found that information out another way."

"Call your brother up. Right now. Have him contact the safe house and have them report that Daddy dear is gone and there's a tied-up cop there who needs rescuing."

But she couldn't call. No phone service. *Tanner could try to text Asher again. Confirm…*

Eli interrupted her thoughts. "A simple exchange. You for him. You come, and I make a phone call and tell the authorities where I stashed your dad."

Mara for her father. She struggled to breathe.

"Climb to the base of the cliffs before sunrise tomorrow. If the cop and the dog come, they die too."

"No."

"No? As in you don't think I can kill them? Didn't we just discuss the fact that you don't give me enough credit? I'm looking at the cop right now. He's coming back around the front with his dog, wearing some ridiculous sweatshirt under his jacket. Easy shot for me. Want me to kill the dog? To give you that proof you're always looking for? Let me just put the radio down for a second…"

"Please, no," she blurted. "Don't hurt them, or my father."

"The only way they live is if you show up tomorrow. Alone. Make your decision." The radio clicked off, leaving her staring at it.

The only way…

It was likely Eli hadn't abducted her father, that it was all a trick. But he knew more than he should and he definitely had a bead on Tanner and Britta. If he didn't get what he wanted he would kill them without a qualm. Her thoughts spun.

The team would arrive, flush Eli out and arrest him.

But their timing was unknown. And Eli would make sure he would cause maximum damage before he was arrested. Holed up in the trees, he could pick the responders off as they arrived—Asher, maybe the new recruits, Willow, Tanner, Britta…her father. Who knew how many would die because Eli didn't get what he wanted...her.

Maybe she could trick him somehow. Get him to spill her father's location and escape. At least stall until the team arrived to back up Tanner. Her throat constricted, as if someone were crushing her windpipe. There was no alternative and she knew it. She could not, would not, let anyone else die. She'd set this whole terrible ball in motion when she'd run instead of trusted her team. Now it was up to her to make it right.

The old grandfather clock chimed as she heard Tanner and Britta entering through the inn's front door. Almost six. Her brain was misfiring, sending jolts of panic and disbelief along her nerves. She knew even without her testimony Eli wouldn't stand a chance of escaping imprisonment no matter what delusions he believed. She was confident in the PNK9 team that they'd craft a tight case, but in Eli's arrogance, he'd imagined a way he could defeat them all. Plus, he blamed her for ruining his plans. Maybe it was no longer a way to escape for Eli, but to exact revenge. He had to make himself a winner no matter what.

She thought back to Eli's comment to Vinny.

"I can pull off Mr. Misunderstood to a jury about the smuggling, but if she takes the stand and convinces them I killed Stacey and Jonas... We'll kill them and bury them somewhere where they'll never be found."

Kill them and bury them somewhere.

Not only her, but Tanner and Britta.

All they'd suffered, the narrow escapes, the excruciating cold, and hunger and injury... Tanner and Britta had endured it all for her. And they'd do it again. Once she told them about the radio message and the sweater, Tanner would order her to stay in the lodge while they marched off to capture Eli. She chewed her thumbnail. Perhaps the team would arrive before dawn.

But if Eli had taken her father and left him without food or medicine, he wouldn't last long, not in his frail condition.

The decision she knew she had to make froze her in place.

Tell Tanner, risk his life to save hers and possibly her father's?

Go alone? Hope she could stall Eli long enough for help to arrive, or maybe come up with a way to save Dad and herself? She caught her own reflection in the mirror, wild-eyed, small, frantic.

The cracked glass of her old watch glimmered in the lamplight. She figured she had about another nine hours to come up with a plan to outwit Eli and sneak out of the inn without Tanner or Britta finding out.

She took a deep breath and spoke the words to herself.

Lord, I will save my father with Your help. I will prevent Eli from taking anyone else's life.

The tap on the door shot her to her feet.

Tanner and Britta entered. "Hey. Do you want to get some dinner? I suspect it's cheese sandwiches again but…" His words trailed off. "What's wrong?"

"I…uh, nothing. Wondering when the team will get here, is all."

"Good question. If I know your brother he's commandeering a helicopter even as we speak."

"Probably." She wiped a bead of sweat from her temple. "I'm not hungry right now, though. You go ahead."

"You sure?"

"One hundred percent. I'm too excited to eat." That part was totally the truth.

He shifted uneasily. "I could bring something up."

With a bright smile, she shook her head. "No appetite. When we get back to Olympia there's a giant burrito with my name on it."

"Okay. Britta will stay with you then."

There was no way she was going to talk him out of leaving the dog on duty.

After another searching look, he let himself out.

Her legs gave way and she sank down on the floor next to Britta. The dog swabbed her face with her tongue, perhaps trying to blot away the anguish she must be able to detect.

"Britta, you have to take care of Tanner, okay?" She blinked back tears. "He's going to need you to be strong for him."

Once he knew what Mara had done…and why she'd done it, he'd understand why she hadn't told him.

Tears rolling down her cheeks, she lay down next to the dog and waited.

THIRTEEN

Tanner blinked awake on the heels of another nightmare, one of several that plagued his sleep.

Mara lying at Vinny's feet, staring at him with pleading eyes. Too late. He'd been too late. He'd dropped to his knees. I'm sorry. And then it wasn't Mara's face he saw but Allie's. She stretched out her hand to him, but he didn't take it. He was paralyzed, an immovable lump, his limbs cemented in place. Breathing hard he sat up, damp with sweat though the room was cold.

Just a dream. With effort, he summoned up a better thought, the memory of him and Allie on the roof of the hospital where he'd been given permission to take her for a picnic of apple juice and soda crackers. He remembered every detail of that visit, the hot wind that smelled of summer, the concentrated sweetness of the apple juice, partially frozen, so cold it made his molars ache. The way her eyes sparkled when she'd felt the sun on her hollow cheeks and a bird skimmed low over the rooftop. Her laughter was like a lush fountain, bubbling out of her decimated body. He'd marveled at it, reveled in it, mourned the loss of it. The illness had stripped her of so many things, but it had never weakened that laugh. He'd felt at the moment so profoundly blessed. She'd squeezed his hand.

"Promise me you won't miss it, Tanny."

"Miss what?"

"All this." She'd twirled in a circle. *"The sun, the sky, every single good moment you can possibly get. Don't miss any of it, do you hear me?"*

He'd swallowed his tears and smiled, not understanding, not really.

But in the last few days with Mara he'd thought maybe he was getting closer to comprehending. Every good moment, every single one, was not to be missed, like the simple pleasure of a hot cup of tea and a shared laugh. He raked his fingers through his overgrown hair, standing it all on end as he wrestled with his thoughts. How could he embrace such joys when the lingering sound of loss still clanged in his ears? Life and death were twined together in mysterious ways only God understood.

His heart thudded in his chest as one thought became clear as a star shining in the winter darkness. Mara was right. He hadn't died with Allie, and she wouldn't have wanted him to.

He healed you so you could keep on living and loving while you're at it.

Living and loving. A smile tugged his mouth. Mara Gilmore was full of life, like her half brother, Asher.

He could almost hear her mischievous chuckle, see the way she pressed her thumbnail to her lower lip when she was thinking something over. The way she challenged him to be a better version of himself. There was so much light in her, like there had been in Allie, the kind that spilled over and lit up the people around her. The twin aches of pain and pleasure made him shake his head. Mara Gilmore had been part of his world since she'd come to Olympia, but it had taken a treacherous scenario for him to see her for who she was…and to see himself.

He closed his eyes and breathed deep. Incredible. He wished he could stay burrowed in that realization and the peace that rippled through him. But it wasn't the proper moment, not yet.

They were hours away from rescue. With the finish line so close, it was dangerous to lose focus and abandon himself to feelings. Their predator was still circling like a vulture. Tanner knew it. Eli hadn't slunk away simply because his henchman had been captured.

He scrubbed a hand over his scruffy chin. He was halfway to having a beard after five days without a shave. Stifling his groan, he rose from the bed. In spite of the painful twinges and tugs, he listened at the adjoining door.

It was early, barely 4:00 a.m., but he heard the shower running in Mara's room, and the murmur of the TV. He didn't blame her for not being able to sleep. Visions of Vinny swam through his waking thoughts, knife plunging down toward her shoulders. But she was fine, he told himself. Alive and well and God had brought them through and He'd see it to the end.

He quietly dressed and checked on Pete and Vinny.

Pete was sleeping in an armchair and Vinny was still unconscious but breathing, the pulse strong in his wrist when Tanner felt for it. True to his word, Pete had assessed him every couple of hours, jotting down the time and Vinny's heart rate, a bottle of water nearby, ready to offer if Vinny roused. His wrist was still loosely cuffed as well as his feet. Best to let them both rest, though he longed to rouse Vinny and ask him to spill information on Eli's whereabouts. The team would roll in as prepared as they could be, but the more info they had ahead of time the safer for everyone. He wished he could be of more help.

Patience, Tanner. He hiked upstairs to the attic and opened the window which let in a frigid blast of wintry darkness that set his eyes watering. He did the bizarre "signal dance" as he'd named it in his head, arcing his body over the balcony railing until he got that one precious bar on his phone.

Vinny in custody at inn. Eli still at large. Send.

After an excruciating couple of seconds, the little swirling dots indicated the message was successfully sent. *Yes*, he thought, pumping his frozen fist.

He waited for a reply until he could barely feel his fingertips and his nose ran from the relentless cold. Nothing. He didn't let it get him down. One way communication was better than nothing. The team would be forewarned that they had one target instead of two. Another encouragement was that no snow was falling and the vicious wind had died away. He'd only been half kidding about Asher acquiring helicopter transport. Clear skies would make it easier if that was the case. The full moon shone unobstructed by storm clouds as the night edged toward morning. All good indications that the roads would be accessible soon. Snowplows were probably already at work. As he reached out to close the windows, something caught his attention in the small pocket of silvery light. A pattern of regular depressions on the snow. Prints left by snowshoes.

Prints?

He blinked to be sure he wasn't seeing things. They led away from the inn toward the trees.

Eli... Every nerve jumped to red alert until logic took over.

The slight depressions were headed *away* from the inn, trailing off toward the snow-laden cliffs. Staring, he could not make out a set of tracks leading *to* the structure. What did it mean?

He pulled the window shut and ran down the steps to the front door. It was unlocked. On the porch step was one pair of snowshoes where there had been two. The tracks he'd spotted had definitely been singular. Made by whom? Not from Pete whom he'd just seen sleeping, and Eli would have left tracks both to and from, even if he'd been the one to take the snowshoes. Vinny was secured and unconscious.

Someone had left the inn. Alone. On snowshoes. Mara was the only possibility. But it couldn't have been her...

He spun back inside taking the stairs two at a time. Mara's door was unlocked.

No. It wasn't possible.

"Mara?" he shouted as he burst through. Now that he was inside, he heard it over the spray of the shower, a steady barking from behind the bathroom door. He shoved it open and Britta sprang out, tail whipping.

"Why were you locked in?" The shower was running, water gone cold. Back in the outer room, he scanned. Mara's backpack was missing.

His stomach plummeted. She'd left. Snuck out and secured Britta so the dog wouldn't alert him.

Why? Why would she have risked falling into the hands of the man who'd vowed to kill her? Disbelief clouded his thinking.

He'd think about her motives on the way. Whatever she was up to, he had to stop her before Eli did.

"Britta," he called but she was already at his side, racing into his room where he helped her step into the harness and booties. It was as if she too knew every moment brought Mara farther away from their protection. *Why, Mara? Why?*

Gear on, they were ready to charge out the door when Pete caught them.

"What? What's going on?"

"Mara's gone."

He frowned. "Gone where?"

"I don't know. My team should be here soon. Keep watch over Vinny until someone comes to relieve you. Won't be long now."

"You sure you don't need backup? Snow's real precarious out there. Avalanche conditions."

"I've got Britta, but thank you." He clasped Pete on the shoulder. "We brought trouble here and I'm sorry for it."

Pete shrugged. "Trouble brought itself. Be safe, Officer Ford."

"I will." He yanked on his hat and gloves as they charged down the stairs. He still could not fathom why she'd gone. On the porch he momentarily considered his options. Returning to get the snowmobile would take him a good hour. Best to go as she did, follow her tracks. While he was strapping on the snowshoes, Britta yipped to get his attention. She shook her ears at him.

His hand went for his gun. He saw nothing except a peaceful white landscape. Britta stared at him. There was something close he needed to look at. Eli?

"Find," he said softly.

Britta sprinted off, nose to the gleaming layer of snow and he clumped along behind. She easily outpaced him. Crouched low, he trailed her. When he caught up she was sitting, laser focused, on a sweater with a patch on the left elbow. The canary yellow was vivid against the frozen background.

That ragged sweater…where had he seen it before?

His stomach balled up. It was the sweater Mara's father had been wearing in the photo Eli had texted her, the one in the keychain photo she carried.

The missing piece clicked into place. Eli had gotten Mara to come to him by making it look like he had her father. Britta's reaction was proof that Eli had handled the garment.

Oh, Mara. You went to save your father? But she was intelligent and savvy, she must have known it could all be a ruse. Why hadn't she trusted him enough to tell him? A flash of hot anger fueled him on.

He was retracing his steps back to her footprints, when his phone buzzed, and then buzzed again and again. Not a text, an actual call! With his teeth he stripped off his glove and answered.

"What's your twenty, Ford?"

"Asher." He heaved out a massive breath. As succinctly as possible he filled Asher in. "I'm in pursuit."

Asher groaned. "Do you have a visual on her?"

"No, but it looks like she's headed up to the base of the cliffs. Britta and I are tracking her now. Where are you?"

"In a snowcat approaching from the east. It was the only vehicle able to tackle the roads since they've not been cleared. I've got the chief and the three rookies with me. We'll meet you there."

"Be advised, it's dangerous. The snowpack is unstable."

Asher paused a beat. "We're talking about an avalanche possibility here?"

"Affirmative."

"Copy that."

He heard a voice from the background whom he recognized as Veronica Eastwood, one of the three candidates vying for a spot on the team.

"Got your GPS tracker online. We can pinpoint your location now, Officer Ford."

"Britta and I are in pursuit. Victim at the lodge needs medical. Call it in."

"Copy that," Asher said.

Only Tanner would recognize the stress underlying Asher's professional tone. Close as he was, he wasn't near enough to help his sister now. He was relying on Tanner to save Mara.

And that's exactly what Tanner intended to do.

Mara's quads ached from her steep ascent. Each step was an effort as she waded through deep pockets of snow. She'd made it to an area thick with towering pines spaced close together. The trees might give her some protection if Eli had a rifle aimed at her from the rocks, but she didn't feel much comfort in it.

He was in control, lying in wait somewhere above in a crevice or cave and she had only a vague plan of escape she'd hastily constructed hours earlier. Did he have her father? She suspected he did not, however, there was no way to be certain and she couldn't take the risk. Eli would make her pay, and more than that, he'd kill Tanner and Britta since they too had thwarted his plan. She clutched the can she'd taken from the reception desk on her way out. Bear spray. The capsaicin-based product would only help if she survived long enough to get close to Eli. Not likely, but it was the one thing she could use in case her other scheme failed.

Twin pinnacles of rock thrust up against the sky which was now a shimmering predawn silver. Tanner had likely discovered what she'd done by now. It killed her to know that he must think her a fool, or believed that she hadn't trusted him to do his job.

It wasn't pride or foolishness or trust. She'd done it to protect the people she loved from a monster. If Eli prevailed and she never left this frozen wilderness, she prayed the team would exact justice anyway by putting him in prison for the rest of his life. Justice for Jonas, Stacey, herself, her father, all the people Eli had hurt.

The air grew thinner, requiring her to stop frequently to catch her breath. Beyond the fringe of trees she could see the base of the cliffs, black gouges in the sparkling granite that marked the location of caves. Plenty of hiding places for Eli. As she panted, a plume of snow peeled away from the cliff face and raced down over the rocks.

Unstable snow, she remembered Pete saying. Climbing around these cliffs was dangerous for so many reasons. The calculator felt bulky in her pocket, key to a ridiculously flimsy plan that might trick Eli, if only for a moment or two. She was probably kidding herself. What kind of a person went off to meet a killer with a can of bear spray and a calculator? *A desperate one.*

Something flicked over her head, and she jumped. Just a bird. How different this would feel if she had Tanner and Britta by her side.

Another dozen arduous steps brought her to the edge of the forest and the bottom of the massive wall of rock. She pressed her back to the rough tree trunk. How could she find Eli? Was he already poised with rifle aimed? Goose bumps erupted on her arms. She brought the radio to her mouth and pressed the button.

"I'm here."

No reply. Another rattle of sliding snow to her left made her jump. What would she do if the snowpack let loose? *Then none of it would matter anyway.*

She tried again.

"You wanted me and I'm here." Again she was met with silence that stoked her into a hot fury in spite of the cold pressing in on her. "All right. I guess you chickened out. I'm leaving."

"What a good little girl," Eli said over the radio, freezing her in place. "But you don't need the radio. I'm closer than you think."

Ripples surged down her spine. *Keep it cool, Mara. You need to get him close.* "Where's my father?" Her gaze roved the swirl of white and black, caves and snow, dizzying.

From out of the blur, Eli appeared, stepping onto a flat rock some twenty feet above her. His rifle was slung over his shoulder. He grinned.

"Thanks for coming, Mara. We could have saved a lot of misery if you'd done this in the first place. You should have taken the fall for Jonas and Stacey."

She glared at him. "Why should I?"

"Because I'm smarter than you. Had to be, to swipe a gun right from the police station out of that shipment slated for destruction. Ruby let slip when the armorer was shipping the weapons. Easy to knock out the power to the utility panel with the tree branch and sneak in. After I killed them and took a few extra shots at the cops and their dogs, I wiped it so it had no prints, but a PNK9 gun could only lead back to you." He grinned, proud of himself.

"You didn't need to kill them."

He shrugged. "They were in my way. And so are you. Come closer. Daddy's waiting."

"I want to know his location. Right now."

"You're not in the driver's seat here, Marbles." He gestured. "Come on. Closer. Now. My patience is wearing thin."

Muscles tight with fear, she unstrapped her snowshoes and stepped out of cover. Eli didn't change positions. He probably wanted her close enough that he couldn't miss. That was exactly what she wanted too.

Trembling all over, she moved to within fifteen feet. "Where's my dad?"

"Old man's pretty feeble," he said, laughing. "Maybe he's passed away, locked up, while you and I have been chatting. Wouldn't that be ironic? You give your life for a dead guy?"

He was toying with her, sticking needles in where he knew it would hurt the most. She took a deep breath. "You're going to tell me where my dad is, and then, if you run real fast, you might get away."

His smile vanished. "You are so full of yourself. You're not the one in charge here." He pulled the rifle to a ready position. "You're the one who's going to die."

Her breath caught. "Sure you don't want to bargain?"

He stopped, squinting. "Bluffing doesn't work for you."

"No bluff." She held up the calculator, careful to conceal it as best she could so all he could see was a rectangular metallic outline. "Satellite phone. I've recorded our conversation. My finger's on the upload button. You tell me about my father or I send the recording along with our precise location to the PNK9 team."

He flinched, then relaxed. "Nice try. You can't get a signal here, even if you had recorded it all, which I doubt."

She smiled. "These mountains are pretty strange, aren't they? Never know when you're going to get a couple of bars. How do you think we contacted the team? They'll be here soon, you know. Sooner, if I press this button."

He grimaced, eyes shining black against the snow. The sun had almost risen, climbing behind the peaks in a cloud of ivory.

"Now that I have your attention," she said, "I want the truth." The seconds ticked by. Would he take the bait?

"Okay. Show of good faith. Put away your phone and I'll show you a photo of where I stashed him."

"Not until you put your rifle down."

He eased it behind his shoulder. "That's as far as it goes."

"Okay. Then my phone comes with me." Gripping the fake, she prayed her ruse would work long enough for her to get within spraying range. Her boots punched into the snow with every step until she reached the rocks. So close now. She could see Eli's knuckles, white against the metal of his weapon, the nervous pinch to his mouth.

He believed she had a phone, or that she might have one. One point in her favor, at least for a few seconds longer.

"My father." She stared at him.

The smug look returned. "He's in a rented house with a friend of mine. Let me see the phone."

The moment had arrived. She forced down the trembling. With her left hand she slowly lifted her pretend phone and with the other, the bear spray.

His eyes widened and he hoisted the rifle with a shout.

She shot the bear spray. The cloud spewed out, but he reeled back and the liquid got him on the temple instead of the face. With a roar, he turned his rifle on her.

She had nowhere to run. She screamed as Eli started to squeeze the trigger.

Tanner and Britta charged out of the trees.

"Get down, Mara."

Eli fired. Chunks of wood flew from the damaged trees as Mara threw herself face-first into the snow.

Noises assaulted her. Britta's charged barking. Gun-shots pinging off the rocky cliff. The roar of a machine. Raising her chin just enough, she saw an awkward-shaped vehicle with a closed cab and massive tank-like tracks instead of tires. It pulled to a stop and the chief and three other people disembarked with another man. Her brother, Asher, and the recruits.

The bullets caused them to take cover as Eli fired.

Tanner returned fire. Eli stumbled, but stayed on his feet.

"Stay where you are," Tanner shouted. He advanced on Eli, moving closer, revolver raised and Britta by his side.

Eli jerked his attention toward the advancing team. He was outmanned and outgunned. Fury twisted his handsome features into something monstrous. He lowered his rifle.

Could they have won?

"I won't be taken to prison," Eli said. He had not yet dropped the rifle.

"No choice." Tanner's gun hand was steady, Britta tense at his side.

She curled up and got her knees underneath her. As she was getting to her feet, the air resounded with a hollow noise, the snow trembling all around them. All around the world began to quiver. The ground slid under her boots.

In disbelief, her brain identified the tumult.

The mountain of snow was barreling down on them.

Avalanche.

FOURTEEN

"Take cover," Tanner shouted.

He saw Eli turn, neck craned toward the patch of snow that broke away from the pinnacle above his head. The crust of white thumped down, collecting more loosened snow until a thunderous river began to surge toward them.

The approaching team scrambled to escape.

The ground rumbled under his feet as he lurched for Mara. She made it to one knee, but the sliding snow impeded her progress. "Hold on." He punched his way through the onslaught. Almost there.

He reached out once. Their fingertips touched and then they were jerked apart. He tried again, calling for Britta. Together he and Britta managed to snag her jacket. They yanked and hauled until they sidestepped the brunt of the flow, moving into the trees.

She would have toppled if Tanner hadn't propped her up behind a sturdy pine.

He pulled Britta between them and looped one arm around a jutting tree branch and the other around her and the dog. If the avalanche increased in size they'd be swept away no matter what actions he took. He clung to her, absorbing the pummeling as much as he could. The snow struck at them with incredible force. Pressed close, he tried to comfort her, tell her it would be okay somehow, but the tumult was deafening, barreling into them with the force of a freight train.

The piling snow crept higher around them. His panic rose along with it. Avalanche deaths were mostly caused by suffocation and hypothermia. He tried to jut out his elbows, to preserve a pocket of air around their heads, but it did no good. The white onslaught fought him, preventing him from doing anything but simply holding on to Mara and Britta as tight as he could.

Just hang on. He wasn't sure if he said the words aloud or in his head. His muscles quaked. His strength was failing. It was only a matter of time before his grip did too.

"Mara," he tried to say again. Was she conscious? Alive?

In a flash, the shuddering stopped, the debris around them steadied. He shoved his shoulders back and forth until he cleared a hollow around them. Britta helped by worming and writhing until she popped out from between them.

"Mara," he gasped, wiping her face clear.

She tipped her head up and blinked ice-glazed lashes at him. Then, at last, the smile that set everything in the world right. In that smile was everything; hope, relief, love, life, faith.

He pressed his forehead to hers as they caught their breath. Speech failed him and he simply listened to her breathing. "I hear the reinforcements coming," he finally managed.

She shifted against him, their lower bodies still immobilized by packed snow. "My dad…"

"We'll sort it out. Soon as they get us loose. Hang on."

She remained still, though he could feel her sobs. Helpless to soothe her, to give her the only thing that would ease her worry, he stayed put, holding back the wall of cold all around them as best he could.

Asher floundered up to them, stopping in a puff of white. The three candidates, Parker, Veronica, Brandie and their dogs accompanied him as well as Chief Fanelli.

"We'll get you out," Asher said.

Veronica stepped forward. She unfolded a shovel and began to loosen the snow. Asher and Parker helped, scooping with their hands.

The other rookie, Brandie, got down on her knees and tunneled from the other side.

Chief Fanelli was on his radio. "Ambulance en route. Where's Eli?"

Tanner shook his head. "I lost him in the avalanche."

"Brandie, put Taz on search. I'll back you up." The chief and Brandie moved away while Veronica and Asher dug away the snow until they were able to pull Tanner and Mara free.

Tanner stretched to his full height and sucked in as much air as he could manage. Before he could check Mara for injuries, Asher grabbed his sister and squeezed her to his chest.

"Dad…" she breathed, choking on tears. "Eli said…"

He pulled her away enough that he could touch her shoulder. "Listen to me. Dad's fine at the safe house.

After Tanner's call, I made contact. It was a ruse. Eli probably took the sweater when he visited."

Sobs wracked her body. "I couldn't take the chance."

"It's okay." Asher cradled her. "Dad's okay."

Tanner had the oddest feeling, a deep sense that he should be the one cradling and comforting Mara. Instead he eased back a step to give them privacy, but he heard anyway.

Mara gulped. "Eli said he'd kill Dad, and Tanner and Britta."

Inwardly, he groaned. She'd gone out to meet Eli partially to protect him and Britta? After he'd hurt her? Turned her away? He stared miserably as Asher once again squeezed his sister close.

"I'm sorry, Mara. I should have trusted you from the get-go, shouldn't have pushed you away because of my anger at Dad."

Mara cried and laid her head against her brother's chest.

Veronica called from a spot in the trees. "Taz has alerted, but we're new at this. He can't pinpoint Eli's location."

Asher released Mara and looked at Tanner. "What about Britta?"

"She's not done a lot of snow work, but I trust her nose."

Asher frowned. "We can bring in an avalanche dog, but it will take some time."

"Let's give her a shot."

Asher nodded. "We'll follow your lead." He gestured to his sister. "Stay here with Veronica. Until we find him, we'll assume he's still a threat."

Tanner concurred. Eli had more lives than a cat. "Britta, find."

Britta zigged and zagged across the snow. She briefly stopped near Veronica and Taz before waggling her way to the base of the rocks. With the massive movement of snow, Eli's scent would be difficult, if not impossible to pick up. Not to mention the whole area was still an unstable mess. He'd give Britta leeway but at the first sign of another avalanche, he'd get his dog and himself to safety. Too many lives had already been lost.

Britta circled twice before settling herself in front of a mound of white. Her brown eyes said it all. *Eli's here.*

At her sit, Tanner drew his weapon. "Here," he called to the team. Before Asher could answer Eli erupted from the snow in a shower of flakes, fumbling for a weapon strapped to his side.

"Stop, Eli," Tanner shouted.

Eli swung the rifle around.

Asher and the chief scrambled to provide cover, Veronica ordering Taz to attack, but Tanner hardly heard. He launched himself at Eli, knocking him into the snow. Britta clamped her teeth around Eli's sleeve, yanking for all she was worth and Taz leaped in also. They struggled only for a moment before help converged and Asher had Eli secured and cuffed.

"Stacey deserved to die," he screamed. "She was going to mess everything up."

Tanner stepped back, breathing hard. Britta pawed his thigh. He pressed his head to hers. "You're the best, Boo Bear."

Britta slurped his neck.

Mara waded through the snow and wrapped her arms

around both of them, tears streaming down her cheeks. "You're okay. Tell me you're both okay. Please."

He steadied his nerves. "Absolutely tip-top."

She pressed her face to his neck. "Is it over?"

He closed his eyes and exhaled, keeping her close, each moment healing him from the inside out. "Yes, Mara. It's over. Finally."

The next few hours unrolled in a blur. The team assembled at the snowcat. Eli was loaded inside. With the chief driving, Asher insisted Mara take the front passenger seat so he could sit in the back and keep eyes personally on the prisoner. There was no worry that Eli would try anything, cuffed, with Brandie and her dog Taz watching his every move, but Tanner understood Asher's decision.

Before the vehicle's doors closed, Tanner tapped on the roof of the snowcat to get Asher's attention. "I'll walk down with Britta. Meet you back at the inn."

Asher frowned. "There's room. We'll squeeze. Don't like you up here with the snow so unsteady."

"We'll be all right."

Asher shot a look at the chief in the rearview. His slight nod indicated he understood.

Tanner felt as if an avalanche had passed through his soul. He needed time alone with his dog to sort through it all.

Asher sighed. "Okay. You've got exactly thirty minutes and then I'm coming up for you."

"Copy that."

The snowcat rumbled away slowly, so as not to create any further disturbances.

When it was gone, Tanner gazed around the terrain

which had only a short time before been menacing and hostile. Now it felt serene, tranquil, as if the mountain had released a terrible burden and found some peace in the aftermath.

"Come on, Britt. Time to put the avalanche behind us."

Ever eager, Britta matched her pace to his as they trudged down the slope.

Mara poured herself another cup of apple cider, letting the steam bathe her face. She'd returned to her job and her cozy apartment in Olympia three weeks prior, but the chill seemed a permanent part of her. She'd probably always have a deep down craving for warm beverages. A Thanksgiving buffet was spread out on a long table in the PNK9 headquarters conference room. A glistening turkey, mashed potatoes, cranberry sauce, stuffing and selection of pies caught the attention of the canines as well as the human officers in the room.

Tanner, with Britta by his side, was talking to Asher. She and Tanner hadn't spent time together since their rescue, except for surface level conversation. They kept it light, chatty. The small talk pained her. All they had shared, endured, been changed by, was in the past. Now she was supposed to think of him as purely a chummy coworker? She turned away.

Danica and Luke stood together, her ring sparkling along with her eyes. She'd been sharing wedding planning tips with Ruby Orton, engaged to Nick Rossi, and Jackson Dean and Everly Lopez. Everly's four-year-old daughter eyed the dogs from her perch on Jackson's shoulders. Everybody was there, sipping cider and talking as Chief Fanelli moved to the head of the table with his old dog, Sarge. Even Isaac and Aubrey had come for the gathering, though Isaac had taken a position with the National Park Police to be closer to Mount Saint Helens, where Aubrey worked. Things had grown less awkward between Mara and the team, as Mara tried to be as forgiving as she hoped they would be. She'd been aloof, they'd been suspicious, but now they were a team again.

Willow clinked her mug with Mara's. "I can't stop staring at you. I'm so over the moon that you're home."

"Me too." Mara couldn't resist hugging her friend, feeling the thickness in her waist. "And I can't take my eyes off your adorable belly."

Willow chuckled, passing a palm over her swollen stomach. "Only another month to go. Theo's repainted the nursery twice because he wasn't happy with the tint."

Mara giggled. "I'm going to have to tease him about that."

The slight lift of Willow's brow indicated she had a question.

"What?"

"Just wondered if anything developed in the romance department between you and Tanner. I always thought you two might have a connection."

Mara's cheeks went molten. "Nothing. Strictly business."

Willow opened her mouth for a follow-up question, but Chief Fanelli clinked his fork to his water glass. "Thanks everyone for coming. I know we've got a ton to be thankful for. Personally, I'm grateful to have the best team of canines and officers in the Pacific Northwest working for me."

There were cheers and whistles.

"Even though," he continued, "some stalwart canine couldn't resist chewing my gym socks in the workout room. Anyone want to confess?"

"They're all taking the fifth," hollered Asher, to more raucous laughter.

"Why am I not surprised?" He laughed. "I've got a good news bulletin for you. Peyton has informed me our recently recovered bloodhounds are suitable for retraining. With a lot of patience and dog treats, they should be part of the team."

Mara joined in the excitement, thrilled to know the puppies had been saved quickly enough to resume their training.

Fanelli nodded and the group quieted. "Anyway, there's an important business item we need to settle, namely, which officers will be given spots on our team. Veronica, Parker and Brandie have been fantastic and the decision hasn't been an easy one."

Mara darted a look at the three who were staring intently at the chief. Sad, that one of them was about to be disappointed, after all they'd done to prove their worth to the team.

Fanelli cleared his throat. "And our decision is…that all three will be invited to join."

The three candidates exchanged bemused glances.

"You've demonstrated your dedication. You've shown you have the heart to join this family. How could we turn any of you away?"

The round of applause was deafening.

Fanelli grinned and raised his water glass. "So how about we grab our plates and load up on some of this amazing food and celebrate together?"

The noise intensified with cheerful congratulations, the clatter of dishware and serving spoons. Mara felt both connected to the merriment and strangely outside it. Suddenly she longed to escape the hubbub, so she quietly exited, making her way to the break area outside.

She inhaled, feeling the Washington sky easing her lungs open as if she was a bird newly released from a cage. She closed her eyes and breathed deeply. When she opened them, her brother stood there, grinning at her.

"You don't need to keep tabs on me anymore," she teased.

"I got some smothering to make up for." Asher looked up at the stars. "Feel strange to be home?"

"Yes and no. I will never take home for granted again, that's for sure."

"And I'll never take my sister for granted either." Asher paused. "I want to say it again. I'm sorry I didn't welcome you into my life. You weren't the problem, I was. All that stuff with Dad and…"

She nodded. "I know that now. Dad's sorry. He asked forgiveness from God."

"Part of me is still angry at what he did to my mom, but the other part…" Now he too breathed deep of the clean mountain air. "If I'm going to accept forgiveness from God, I have to dole it out too, don't I?"

She smiled at her handsome brother. "That's the deal."

He hugged her and she clung to him for a moment. Her brother…another blessed gift from the Lord.

"Peyton is going full bore on the planning now that

you're back home. I hope you and Tanner will be at our wedding."

She played with the zipper on her jacket. "We will be." *Just not as a couple.*

He arched his brow. "Do I detect a little discomfort about the subject of you and Tanner?"

"There is no 'me and Tanner.'"

"Are you sure?"

"Yes."

His silence made her cheeks burn.

"Okay. I can take a hint. Stay in your lane, brother." The door slid open, and Tanner poked his head out.

Now her discomfort swelled to epic levels.

"Am I interrupting?" he asked.

Yes, she wanted to say.

"Not at all. I was just going to find Peyton." Asher gave Tanner a smack on the back before he departed.

Britta pranced over to Mara, bottom waggling and a ball in her mouth. She laughed and hurled it for her. Britta raced off in hot pursuit.

"That party was getting noisy." Tanner's hands were jammed into the pockets of his neat khakis, his dark polo shirt borrowing the brown hue of his eyes. "Feeling okay?"

"Sure. Completely. I have some aches and pains but they're hardly a blip on the radar." She hoped her tone was sufficiently upbeat. With him standing there, she simply did not know how to act. *Chummy colleagues, remember?* "It's nice to hear how everyone's life has progressed while I've been gone."

"Yeah. So much has changed."

"That's for sure. Engagements, marriages, babies, and now three new recruits."

"Uh-huh."

The silence stretched between them before Tanner cleared his throat. "I uh, I'm going to make some changes too."

"Oh, yeah? Tell me about them." Britta returned and plopped the ball at Mara's feet. She chucked it again for the dog.

"I'm going to buy that piece of land after the holidays are over. Off-the-grid, like I told you. Dogs, a garden, the works."

The disappointment curled like smoke in her belly. "Just like you and Allie dreamed of."

"Yes, and no. I decided to look closer to home, to the Mount Rainier area. Plenty of wild acres around here to build a place. And I like my job." He shifted. "Time to dream a new dream, instead of trying to hang on to an old one."

She couldn't hold back her surprise. "Oh. That's… good. Right?"

"Yes. I wasn't ready before. I was still holding on to the pain. I've decided God's trying to tell me there will always be pain, but that doesn't mean you can't have joy too." He nudged her with an elbow. "Someone smart showed me that."

She blinked back a sudden wash of tears. "I'm glad that someone was able to help."

"I didn't think the two could coexist, pain and joy. I think maybe I didn't want them to. There's something about holding your pain close, like it's a blanket or a Kevlar vest. Nothing else can get through and that feels safe."

"Nothing is safe." She breathed deep again. "That's what I've learned. Nothing is safe, or guaranteed on this earth." *Not life, not love.* When her throat thickened, she forced a happy tone. "That's why I'm going to sop up every moment God sees fit to give me and do my best to be grateful for it."

Britta sprinted back, dropped the ball at Mara's feet with a cheerful yip.

She flung it again, Britta tracking the wide arc through the sky as she ran to receive it. Mara turned to find Tanner staring at her, his face serious. "Can we… do that together?"

"Do what?"

"Enjoy the moments He gives us."

Mara cocked her head. "I'm not sure what you're asking."

"I want to be with you, wherever God takes us. You and me, together."

She gaped, stunned and mute. What had she just heard him say?

He shifted. "I had this new dream see…that someday we could share an off-the-grid life together. Or whatever type of life you want to try." He was looking at the sky now, the clouds reflected in his irises. "I love you, Mara." The words were soft as the clouds.

He loved her? Her breathing hitched. For a moment, she thought she was imagining him saying what her own heart was silently shouting. How could it be happening? To her? With him?

He turned to face her and took her hands.

"You fill up my heart and I thought it would be empty forever. You showed me it's not empty and it never will be. Allie is still there, in the place she belongs. But you belong there too because I've never met such a brave, honest, intelligent woman. We could build a dream together. A different one, whatever we decide will make you happy too."

Dream. That was what this was. A dream.

But he squeezed her fingers, drawing her closer so his warmth bled into hers. "I've lost a lot of time pushing away the blessings God was trying to give me, and I'm not going to do that again." He looked at her now. "I love you, Mara. Do you think you can grow to love me too?"

A breeze trickled through her body, wafting away the shadows of grief, quickening her heart into a new rhythm. "I already do love you," she choked out.

His smile dazzled her as he swept her into a fierce hug. Britta barked and danced around them. He set her down and kissed her breathless.

She was so bursting with fierce happiness she almost missed his next words.

"The first thing I want to do is meet your father."

Her vision blurred with exquisite tears. "You do?"

His smile was wide, certain. "I've got a question to ask him."

"I'm not sure he'll…understand," she whispered.

"He deserves to be asked anyway."

She did not think she could love Tanner Ford more, but her heart swelled until it seemed as if her body might not contain it.

"So what do you say, Mara Gilmore? Want to go

on the run with me and Boo Bear? I can't promise you backpack pancakes, but we'll do our best to make you happy."

She threw her arms around him and held him tight. "Why yes, Officer Ford. I believe I will."

* * * * *

Dear Reader,

Whew! What a ride! This PNK9 team has been through some big adventures and it's not over yet! The series continues with two more novellas that you're going to love. I had a lot of fun writing this book because it is literally a "running for your life" story. Personally, I can't imagine surviving for seven months as a fugitive, being tracked by a killer, can you? I have trouble finding my car at the mall! Talk about no survival instincts. If I was in Mara's shoes, I'd sure be grateful to have Tanner and Britta show up. In spite of storms, hunger, injury and two killers tracking their every move, they worked together to get back home…just in time for Thanksgiving!

Thank you so much for reading my story and all the other wonderful books in the PNK9 series. I hope you and your family will be richly blessed this holiday season.

Fondly,
Dana Mentink

Get 3 FREE REWARDS!

We'll send you 2 FREE Books plus a FREE Mystery Gift.

FREE
Value Over
$20

Both the **Love Inspired®** and **Love Inspired®** Suspense series feature compelling novels filled with inspirational romance, faith, forgiveness and hope.

YES! Please send me 2 FREE novels from the Love Inspired or Love Inspired Suspense series and my FREE gift (gift is worth about $10 retail). After receiving them, if I don't wish to receive any more books, I can return the shipping statement marked "cancel." If I don't cancel, I will receive 6 brand-new Love Inspired Larger-Print books or Love Inspired Suspense Larger-Print books every month and be billed just $6.49 each in the U.S. or $6.74 each in Canada. That is a savings of at least 16% off the cover price. It's quite a bargain! Shipping and handling is just 50¢ per book in the U.S. and $1.25 per book in Canada.* I understand that accepting the 2 free books and gift places me under no obligation to buy anything. I can always return a shipment and cancel at any time by calling the number below. The free books and gift are mine to keep no matter what I decide.

Choose one: ☐ **Love Inspired**   ☐ **Love Inspired**   ☐ **Or Try Both!**
             Larger-Print   **Suspense**   (122/322 & 107/307
             (122/322 BPA GRPA)   **Larger-Print**   BPA GRRP)
                                        (107/307 BPA GRPA)

Name (please print)

Address   Apt. #

City   State/Province   Zip/Postal Code

Email: Please check this box ☐ if you would like to receive newsletters and promotional emails from Harlequin Enterprises ULC and its affiliates. You can unsubscribe anytime.

Mail to the Harlequin Reader Service:
IN U.S.A.: P.O. Box 1341, Buffalo, NY 14240-8531
IN CANADA: P.O. Box 603, Fort Erie, Ontario L2A 5X3

Want to try 2 free books from another series! Call 1-800-873-8635 or visit www.ReaderService.com.

HARLEQUIN
PLUS

Try the best multimedia subscription service for romance readers like you!

Read, Watch and Play.

Experience the easiest way to get the romance content you crave.

Start your **FREE TRIAL** at
<u>www.harlequinplus.com/freetrial</u>.

LOVE INSPIRED

Stories to uplift and inspire

DISCOVER.

SCAN ME

Get exclusive content and be the first to find out about promotions and other news!
LoveInspired.com

EXPLORE.

SCAN ME

Sign up for the Love Inspired e-newsletter and download a free book at
TryLoveInspired.com

CONNECT.

Join our Love Inspired community to share your thoughts and connect with other readers!

 Facebook.com/LoveInspiredBooks

Twitter.com/LoveInspiredBks

LIIBC2022-R

LOVE INSPIRED SUSPENSE
INSPIRATIONAL ROMANCE

To rescue a witness…

this K-9 team must face a killer and a storm.

After months tracking a colleague falsely accused of ...er Ford and his K-9 partner ...more—but the real murderer ...they must run into a frozen wilderness to ...urvive. Evading the killer is the only way for Mara to clear ...er name. But will the harsh winter conditions cover their ...racks...or bury them forever?

A PACIFIC NORTHWEST K-9 UNIT NOVEL

CATEGORY: **SUSPENSE**

$6.75 U.S./$7.75 CAN.

ISBN-13: 978-1-335-59768-7

5 0 6 7 5

9 781335 597687

EAN

Ⓢ

Courage.
Danger.
Faith.

LOVE INSPIRED
LoveInspired.com